DARKBOUND

Michaelbrent
COLLINGS

There is no light at the end of some tunnels....

For more information on Michaelbrent's books, including specials and sales; and for info about signings, appearances, and media,

check out his webpage,

"Like" his Facebook fanpage
or
Follow him on Twitter.

PRAISE FOR THE NOVELS OF
MICHAELBRENT COLLINGS

THE HAUNTED

"*The Haunted* is a terrific read with some great scares and a shock of an ending!" – Rick Hautala, international bestselling author; Bram Stoker Award® for Lifetime Achievement winner

"[G]ritty, compelling and will leave you on the edge of your seat.... *The Haunted* is a tremendous read for fans of ghoulishly good terror." – horrornews.net

"*The Haunted* is just about perfect.... This is a haunted house story that will scare even the most jaded horror hounds. I loved it!" – Joe McKinney, Bram Stoker Award®-winning author of *Flesh Eaters* and *Inheritance*

APPARITION

"*Apparition* is not just a 'recommended' novel, it is easily one of the most entertaining and satisfying horror novels this reviewer has read within the past few years. I cannot imagine that any prospective reader looking for a new read in the horror genre won't be similarly blown away by the novel." – *Hellnotes*

"[*Apparition* is] a gripping, pulse hammering journey that refuses to relent until the very final act. The conclusion that unfolds may cause you to sleep with the lights on for a spell.... Yet be forewarned perhaps it is best reserved for day time reading." – horrornews.net

"*Apparition* is a hard core supernatural horror novel that is going to scare the hell out of you.... This book has everything that you would want in a horror novel.... it is a roller coaster ride right up to a shocking ending." – horroraddicts.net

"[*Apparition* is] Riveting.   Captivating.   Mesmerizing....   [A]n effective, emotional, nerve-twisting read, another amazingly well-written one from a top-notch writer." – *The Horror Fiction Review*

THE LOON

"It's always so nice to find one where hardcore asylum-crazy is done RIGHT.... *THE LOON* is, hands down, an excellent book." – *The Horror Fiction Review*

"Highly recommended for horror and thriller lovers. It's fast-moving, as it has to be, and bloody and violent, but not disgustingly gory.... Collings knows how to write thrillers, and I'm looking forward to reading more from him." – *Hellnotes*

MR. GRAY (AKA THE MERIDIANS)

"... an outstanding read.... This story is layered with mystery, questions from every corner and no answers fully coming forth until the final conclusion.... What a ride.... This is one you will not be able to put down and one you will remember for a long time to come. Very highly recommended." – *Midwest Book Review*

HOOKED: A TRUE FAERIE TALE

"*Hooked* is a story with depth.... Emotional, sad, horrific, and thought provoking, this one was difficult to put down and now, one of my favourite tales." – *Only Five Star Book Reviews*

"[A]n interesting and compelling read.... Collings has a way with words that pulls you into every moment of the story, absorbing every scene with all of your senses." – *Clean Romance Reviews*

"Collings has found a way to craft an entirely new modern vampire mythology – and one strikingly different from everything I've seen before.... Recommended for adult and teen fans of horror and paranormal romance...." – *Hellnotes*

RISING FEARS

"The writing is superb. The characters are believable and sympathetic... the theme of a parent who's lost a child figures strongly; it's powerful stuff, and written from the perspective of experience that no one should ever have to suffer." – *The Horror Fiction Review*

Other Books by Michaelbrent Collings

The Haunted

Apparition

The Loon

Rising Fears

Mr. Gray (aka The Meridians)

Hooked: A True Faerie Tale

Billy: Messenger of Powers (The Billy Saga, Book 1)

Billy: Seeker of Powers (The Billy Saga, Book 2)

6 FARES

5 FARES

4 FARES

3 FARES

2 FARES

6 FARES

Maddie told me she wants to live in Sleeping Beauty's Castle someday. I told her that was a bad idea, because she'd be asleep the whole time and wouldn't be able to enjoy it.

She told me she wasn't worried about that; that she knew I would come and wake her up with a kiss. I smiled and kissed her right then and she asked if that kiss would keep her awake and I told her yes so she asked if she could stay up late and watch a movie. I think she had that in mind the whole time. Crafty little fox.

ONE

Jim's first indicator that he should have waited for the next subway was the skull driving the train.

But no, that was wrong, wasn't it? Because it happened even before that. It came when Jim was holding the picture. Looking at the picture of his two girls, wishing that he hadn't fought with them.

Maddie was looking at her mother, looking at Carolyn, both of them smiling at each other like they didn't have a care in the world, like there was no such thing as sickness or disease or bills or even so much as the occasional shortage of a favorite sugared cereal. Just them. Just love.

No family fights. No angry words. No misunderstandings. No remorse.

Then Jim smelled it. Smelled it before he saw it.

The smell was sweet. But not pleasant. Sweets, as any post-Halloween child could tell you, were great to a point. After that, though, they were nauseating. And, indeed, Jim immediately felt sick as an almost overpowering smell of bubble gum and lollipops and sourballs and Skittles and Starburst and a hundred other kinds of candy that he couldn't define wafted into his face.

"Pretty," said the voice.

Jim looked toward the sound. He felt his nose and mouth wrinkling in disgust at the smell of sickly sweetness.

He tried to stop it from happening, but couldn't. Some fights couldn't be won, some emotions couldn't be hidden, not even by someone who was trained as he was.

"Sorry?" he said. And his mouth was still curled, so much so that the word sounded less like he was apologizing for failing to hear and more like he was issuing a threat. Like he was on the verge of punching the man who had spoken.

Maybe he was.

In his travels through life, Jim had found that there were a few, a very *unlucky* few, who engendered immediate disgust bordering on hatred in others. And the hunched, ferret-eyed, balding man beside him had just that effect. He was wearing a trench coat, the official garb of pedophiles and flashers everywhere, and Jim couldn't help notice the strange stains that turned it from tan to brown in certain spots. The mousy man looked like he was about thirty-five, though he had the balding pate and bad comb-over of a man who could be as old as fifty. Hard to tell with some people.

"I said she's pretty," said the man. He was eating some kind of colorful candy, and had a purple half-chewed lollipop in one sticky-looking hand.

Geez, thought Jim, this guy is diabetes waiting to happen.

Then he realized that the guy was still looking at the picture he held. At his girls. At Carolyn.

At Maddie.

Maddie was only seven, and the picture was small. No way to tell just by the other guy's eyes exactly who he was looking at. And Carolyn was a knockout, no doubt

3

about it. So most red-blooded males that Jim had ever met would no doubt be drooling over the mother in the picture.

But not this guy. No. Jim's hackles raised. He had experience with guys like this. He knew. He could just *tell*.

He pulled the picture away from the man. Slowly. Like he was someone who had somehow found himself standing naked in front of a hungry lion while holding a piece of bloody meat.

The other man's eyes tracked the picture hungrily. He put the lollipop in his mouth. "Pretty," he mumbled around the sucker, and then slurped on it as Jim put the picture into the small journal he always carried with him. He put the book into his pocket. A tight fit, but it went in.

"Thanks," said Jim. He tried to say it in a way that would communicate "Don't take this personally but leave me the hell alone."

His new friend didn't seem to get it. The man grinned around lips that had been stained cadaver blue by the lollipop and then shoved out his hand. "Fred," he said. "Fred Piper, but everyone just calls me Fred – Freddy, actually."

The air, already almost unbreathable due to the heavy smell of sweets, now seemed almost toxic. Jim felt like he might pass out. It was only the thought of Fred-Piper-Fred-Freddy-Actually rifling through his pockets and removing the picture from Jim's journal that kept him from going over in a nauseated faint.

He managed to stay upright, but beyond that he didn't know what to do.

Jim looked around. It was early, so there were hardly any people on the platform with them.

Closest to Jim: a stunningly beautiful woman with dark hair. She held a leather satchel and wore expensive clothes and four hundred dollar high-heeled boots. Looked like she was probably one of the high-priced midtown Manhattan lawyers that worked ungodly hours in return for bragging rights, a cramped apartment, and the hope of making partner someday. And, of course, those boots. Totally impractical winter wear, but they screamed money. Jim knew that was important to some people.

Just past her stood a thick-necked black man whose dark sweater and winter coat couldn't quite hide the gang tattoos that curled up his neck before disappearing under the heavy knit hat that covered most of his head. Not to mention the four black tears tattooed directly below his right eye. Jim knew from his work what those meant: one tear for every gang-confirmed kill: the equivalent of painting an "x" on the side of his plane during World War II. Only the war this man had – or still – fought in was a gloomier, more unruly war than that fought by the Greatest Generation. A war fought with drive-by shootings and beat-downs in alleys, with rapes of rivals' cousins and sisters and wives, with Molotov cocktails tossed into ramshackle tenements where firefighters dared not go.

A few feet beyond the gangbanger was another man who was even larger and who somehow seemed to Jim even more dangerous: a white man with a spear-bald head. He looked like he was in his late forties or early fifties, and though he wore only a white button-up shirt and a light suit coat, he seemed utterly immune to the late autumn chill that had made its way even down to the underground subway platform. His forehead was a wide block that looked like it had been formed from an exceptionally ill-tempered piece of granite. His nose was crooked and flattened: broken more than once. His eyes stared straight ahead, but Jim felt certain that the man was not only aware of everyone on the platform, but could also tell where the exits were, where the phones were, and everything else of tactical importance.

Jim knew there would be no help from any of them.

New Yorkers weren't actually the jerks that many comedians and television shows made them out to be. Jim found most of them to be pleasant and helpful. But there were exceptions, and he didn't get a "Just call and I'll be there" feel off of any of the folks on the platform. More a "Just call and I'll help whoever's mugging you to hold you down and then we'll split the take" kind of vibe.

All this observation took only a moment. Less. A split-second. Even so, Freddy was starting to jitter, like the trench coat-wearer was considering throwing himself at Jim for not answering him fast enough. He had given his name, and it was clear he expected to get Jim's name – his *full* name – in return. Not to mention a discussion of the "pretty" girl in the picture now safe in the journal in Jim's pocket.

And that was something Jim had no intention of getting into. No intention of engaging this creepy guy in a conversation about *anything*, let alone about a discussion of Carolyn or Maddie. Especially Maddie.

But what *should* he say?

He looked around again.

And then Freddy jumped. He yelped. Jim thought for a second that the crazy guy was going to jump on him, then realized that the short shout had been one of pain. At the same moment the weasel, who had been holding his half-chewed lollipop when he screamed, also jumped up. He jerked convulsively and his lollipop punched upward into his mouth. He screamed this time as the jagged shards of the candy rammed through the top of his soft palate.

"Ow!" he yelled. He spit, and candy fragments and blood came out. Jim almost smiled. Almost. But didn't. He was still too freaked out. And now worried as well. What had just happened?

A moment later he had his answer as Freddy whipped around, revealing a short, portly woman. Jim hadn't seen her on the subway platform: she must have been exactly behind Freddy. But when the man turned he could see her easily. She looked like she was in her seventies, probably Hispanic, dressed from head to toe in black. She stared up at Freddy from all of five feet three inches of *latina* fury.

"You go away!" she hollered, her voice thickly accented with the warm tones of tropical upbringing. "No one wants you here!"

"What right do you have –?" began Freddy. Then Jim found out what had caused the creep to jump and stab himself with his candy in the first place as the older woman unleashed a quick double kick with her right foot, slamming a thick orthopedic shoe into each of Freddy's shins.

"Shut up," she shouted, punctuating each word with a kick. "Go away, pervert."

"*Pervert?*" Freddy looked genuinely horrified. "I'm no pervert. I think kids are... they're *angels*. They're

7

perfect *angels*. I coach the soccer team for Christ's – Ow!"
He broke into another scream as the old lady tagged him
with another kick.

"Don' you take the Lord's name in vain!" she said,
shaking a withered finger in his face as Freddy hopped
from one foot to another as though unsure which one
deserved more babying. It was a comical scene, and one
that Jim would have laughed at if he hadn't been so close to
freaking out less than a second ago: the pedophile being
faced down by the black-clad old lady who looked like
some bizarre escapee from a Mexican ninja training camp,
said pedophile doing the hokey-pokey while desperately
trying to salvage what remained of his lollipop.

"What the hell's *wrong* with – *ow!*"

Another kick.

"You gonna curse, too?" shrieked the old woman.
"You one of those naughty boys who needs to be all 'F this'
and 'A that' and 'Double-S on those'?" More kicks. *Bam-
bam-bam.* Her voice was starting to rise, moving toward a
hysterical shriek, and Jim wondered if Freddy might not be
the only crazy on the subway platform: the old lady
seemed like she might have a bagful of cats hidden
somewhere nearby – or maybe it was an invisible bag and
she was already holding it.

Then Jim saw her eyes. There was a twinkle in
them. She was *enjoying* herself. And not in the maniacal
way that the crazies did, not in the way of those who
belonged to the Cult of the Tinfoil Hats and
Commandeered Brainwaves. No, he could see now that
this little woman was in total control of herself. But she
had found someone who needed a bit of a talking-to – or

shin-kicking – and having found such a person, she was enjoying herself immensely.

Jim started to smile, the look coming over him unconsciously, but she caught his gaze and gave the smallest shake of her head – a motion so minute that he was certain no one else could have detected it. He understood instantly: it was one thing for *him* to know what she was doing. But if they were to get rid of Freddy, this had to seem serious.

The *latina* kept kicking at the geek, flailing at his legs with her heavy leather footwear until he retreated across the platform. He veered away from the beautiful woman like she was a Gucci-wearing cattle prod. That wasn't surprising, Jim thought: many pedophiles were threatened by anyone who was assured, confident-seeming. It was one of the reasons they turned to children in the first place: they knew they could bully them into subservience, into silence, into invisibility and ultimately into dissolution.

Freddy moved toward the black guy, but the gangbanger cracked his knuckles and that was enough to send the geek scuttling away, past the gangbanger and then the huge white man, until he had practically disappeared in the shadow of a supporting column at the far end of the platform.

Jim felt sick. He wished there was something he could call the cops about. Something he could get Freddy in trouble for. But what was he going to do? Call 911 and then say, "Yes, I'd like to report a man looking at a picture of my little girl"? That would just get *him* in trouble. And he didn't want that, either.

He looked away from Freddy. Back to the Hispanic gal. She was still staring at Freddy, looking at the man who was now all but hidden in the shadows at the other end of the platform like he was a dangerous life form.

That's not far off, thought Jim.

There was no doubt in his mind Freddy *was* a child molester. He had all the signs. Not just the outfit, but other things. He was fixated on sweets, he had a childlike way of expressing himself. He spoke of children in terms that were over-idyllic, almost worshipful. Looking at him was like looking at a textbook of pedophilia made flesh.

Without looking away from the creep, the old woman said, "I see him looking at your picture. I don't like him."

"I don't like him, either."

The air on the platform changed. It was hard to explain to someone who had never experienced it, but you could almost *feel* the subway train approaching. Certainly there was sound, but even before that the atmosphere got heavier, as though the train was pushing the air before it and compressing the air on the platform, so you were bearing up under more than usual. And yet at the same time you could feel oxygen sucking out of your lungs. Pushing, pulling, pulling, pushing. It was an impossible set of contradicting experiences, but they were real.

Then the sound came, a rushing noise, the sound of electricity humming and crackling a thousand times a second, the sound of metal wheels on metal tracks that had borne such loads a million million times and would do so a million million more.

Jim was traveling a path he traveled every day. So he'd done his "pre-walking" – a term that some New Yorkers used to describe getting to the part of the subway train that would have them disembarking the subway at the point closest to the gate they needed. Doing so saved precious moments in a place where every second seemed to count far too much.

In Jim's case, doing so meant he had taken a position at the end of the platform closest to the place where the subway would emerge from the tunnel. That was why he only got the quickest glimpse of the driver. If he'd been standing at the other end of the platform – where Freddy was sulking, or even where the gangbanger or the big man or the lawyer were standing – he would have been able to see it longer.

But not here. Not at the very spot where the train emerged. Here he just saw it for a split-second.

Jim looked over at his tiny savior, at the feisty Hispanic woman who had rescued him from the unwelcome attentions of Freddy. He didn't know why he looked at her.

No, that's a lie, Jim. Don't do that. Don't lie to yourself. You're looking to see if she saw it, too.

There was no way. No way she would have seen it. No way she *could* have seen it. There was nothing *to* see.

But as Jim looked, the woman crossed herself. She touched her fingers to her lips and kissed them and whispered something under her breath. Then she turned her face to him – a face grown noticeably paler in the last second – and said, "Did you see it? Did you see the demon?"

TWO

Jim shook his head. "No. No, I didn't see a demon."

But then what *had* he seen?

He looked at the woman again, the little woman who had seemed so imperturbable only a moment before, who had faced down someone that Jim knew in his gut was undoubtedly a child molester without so much as blinking an eye. Now she was sweating visibly, even in the cold winter air.

Think, Jim. Just be calm, just think.

The train had come out of the tunnel. It had come out like it always did, with that sound like an ocean wave in need of oiling, with that rush of hot-cold air that push-pulled the wind around it. Everything normal.

Except the skull.

The trains on this line ran with a driver, who sat in a small compartment at the front of the lead car. The compartment was sealed off from the rest of the train –

Thank you very much, 9/11!

– but you could see the driver's face and torso through the small window that was just to one side of the subway car's center line. The drivers came in all shapes and sizes: fat, thin, tall, short, white, black, Asian, Hispanic, and everything in between.

But this driver…. This one had been different. He'd been wearing the usual outfit. The usual reflective vest. The usual MTA transit hat that always looked to Jim like it was somehow stuck in a place halfway between "quaint" and "obsolete."

But below the hat, where Jim should have seen a face, should have seen a bored New York expression readying itself for one more leg of an endless-seeming shift, he saw only pale white bone, a fleshless skull. The skull swiveled toward him in the instant the subway train emerged from the tunnel. The eyes were black, and the train passed so fast that Jim shouldn't have been able to seen any detail.

But he did. Or at least, he saw an *impression* of detail.

Snakes. Bodies writhing. Liquid pouring over mouths agape and drowning. A fire that was hot but did not warm, flames that burnt but at the same time snuffed out all light. All these Jim thought he glimpsed in the skull's eye sockets, in those black pits above the widely grinning teeth and hollow nasal cavity.

Then it was past. Gone. A piece of memory. Imagination.

Impossibility.

"The demon," repeated the old woman beside him. "Did you see it?"

Jim forced a smile onto his face. "No." And as he said it, it became real. So many things can be forced away through the power of denial. Even truth.

"He looked like...." She crossed herself again. "He looked like a skull."

"Probably just a skinny guy and some bad morning lighting. Plus I haven't had my first coffee of the day yet, so I just assume *anything* I see is bad lighting."

The woman looked at him with naked hope in her eyes. "You think?"

"I know," he said. And then, as much to take his mind and the conversation away from what he had just seen, he offered his arm. "I'm Jim."

The woman almost fell onto him. She wrapped both arms around his for a moment, then seemed to remember her dignity. She straightened and let one of her hands fall away from him, though she kept her closest arm twined through the crook of his elbow. "Adolfa," she said. She said something else, perhaps her last name, but the train shrieked to a halt and he didn't hear it.

"Charmed," he said, and tipped an imaginary hat to her before leading her toward the train. "Back car all right?"

She nodded. Jim looked over. Gorgeous lawyer, gangbanger, scary white dude, and Freddy the Perv all looked like they were headed for different train cars. Which was fine by Jim. None of them seemed like the kind of people he wanted to sit down and share secrets or become Bestest Friends with at the moment.

He led Adolfa to the doors of the back car. Or better said, he *tried* to lead her: about halfway there he realized that *she* was actually leading *him*. Realizing this, and reflecting on how she had handled Freddy, he wondered if he would be able to take her in a prize fight, best two out of three. He decided an experienced Bronx bookie would give him the edge, but only barely.

The doors of the back car slid open. He waited for the current passengers to disembark, then saw that there was no one in the car.

"Never seen *that* before," he said.

"What?"

Jim almost leapt out of his shoes. He hadn't been aware he had spoken aloud. "The car. It's early, but usually there are at least a *few* people getting off."

Adolfa smiled. She patted his arm with her free hand. "More privacy for us, *mi hijo*."

He grinned at her. "You flirting with me?"

She waved him away with a gesture that managed to be both playful and prim. "*Ay*, no. You're too old for me."

Jim laughed at that, then stepped into the train car. He looked over. The next car could be seen through the dividing doors. A few people in it, maybe ten or twelve.

"This must be the car for the lower class," he said.

"No," said Adolfa. Gesturing to the commuters in the other car, she added, "This is far too *exclusivo* for them. None of them could afford this place."

Jim laughed again. He liked this old gal. He waved grandly, a sweeping bow toward one of the plastic chairs that was held to the wall partly by bolts and epoxy, partly by hardened gum. "Please do sit, milady." He did his best to affect an upper-crust accent, but suspected it came out sounding like Thurston Howell from *Gilligan's Island*, if good ol' Thurston had just had a root canal.

Adolfa sat down. She immediately leaned over to massage her calves. Grimacing, she said, "Don't get old."

"I don't think I'll be able to avoid it."

She looked like she was going to respond, but there was a double tap of heels on metal as someone came into the car. Jim and Adolfa both looked at the sound and saw the gorgeous woman enter the car, the high heels of her expensive boots ringing sharply on the subway flooring. She barely glanced at them before moving halfway down the car. She leaned against a support pole and immediately began texting on her cell phone.

Jim was struck again by how beautiful the woman was. Not like his Carolyn – no one was like her – but beautiful, nonetheless. She was dark, with olive skin and eyebrows that were thick without being bushy. Her hair was lustrous and hung in waves to a point just past her shoulders. She reeked of class. Money. A girl on the move, on the make.

Jim looked back at Adolfa. The old woman was also looking at the newcomer. "Pretty," said Adolfa.

"Very."

"Why she not get on the other car, I wonder?"

Jim shrugged. He would have pointed out that asking a New Yorker about their choice of subway car was definitely against the unspoken etiquette book that every person in the city somehow had downloaded into their brains within their first month of residency, but suspected that Adolfa already knew that.

Another set of hollow thumps announced the entry of another passenger onto the train car.

It was the gangbanger. He entered the car with a grunt that spoke of his annoyance and clearly communicated the fact that this wasn't his first choice of travel accommodations. Like the lawyer, though, he moved past Jim and Adolfa before either of them could have spoken even if they *were* so inclined.

And right behind him was the huge white man. Up close he was even more formidable than he had previously appeared. At first, Jim had taken him for a meatpacker who'd made good. Now, he realized that the man looked more like a dock worker. His face was tough and leathery, though not suntanned. Indeed, he wasn't tanned at all. No, what gave his skin its leathery impression was the fact that it was criss-crossed with dozens of thin scars, as though someone had gone at him with an extremely fine razor blade long ago.

The huge man ducked to get through the doors. His eyes flicked up and down the subway car, took in its occupants in an instant, then he sat down across the aisle from Adolfa and Jim. He closed his eyes. Jim had the impression, though, that the man was about as asleep as a member of a bomb squad working on defusing a tactical nuke with a hole-punch and a Swiss Army Knife.

Two softer thuds pulled Jim's attention away from the big man. He looked over to the still-open subway doors –

(*why are they still open, they* never *stay open this long, how long are we going to wait before we just get going?*)

– but even before he shifted his gaze, he knew what he'd see. Freddy.

17

Adolfa started to stand, and Jim could see from the murderous gleam in her eyes that another round of shin-kicking was in the offing.

Freddy must have seen it, too, because his hands went up. "Whoa, whoa," he said. A disgusting whine had crept into his voice. "Do you think I *want* to be here?" His voice cracked in the middle of the question. Jim smelled the man's odor, that candy-infused scent, and had to concentrate on quelling the nausea that accompanied it. He didn't want to add the reek of vomit to the air.

Freddy took a nervous chew of his lollipop, which by now was little more than a white paper stick with a ragged purple ring on the top. He gestured with it to the platform outside. "All the other cars are stuck," he said.

"What?" said Jim.

"Stuck," repeated Freddy. "The doors won't open."

"Baloney," said Adolfa. The word sounded funny coming from her, but the look in her eyes was anything but. She started to stand again.

Freddy's hands started waving frantically. He could have taken first place in a jazz-hands competition. "No, I swear, I swear," he said. He took a half-step back, seemed to realize that would have him outside the subway car, then moved back in. "None of the other doors opened."

"Ba-lo-ney," repeated Adolfa. She pulled herself fully upright, using a pole for support. Or maybe, Jim thought, she was just getting ready to use it as extra leverage to kick Freddy the Perv off the train.

"Is true," said a deep voice.

Jim looked at the older man across the car. His eyes were still closed, his thick arms crossed across a barrel chest. But it was definitely him who had spoken. And he did so again. His voice was seeped in an accent that Jim couldn't quite place. He thought it might be Russian, or perhaps Armenian or Hungarian. Certainly something from that neck of the woods. "Is why we get on this car. Other doors refused open."

"How is that possible?" Jim said. He looked down the car's length, through the dividing doors; saw the dozen or so commuters in the other car. "How did *they* get in the car?"

The huge man cracked a single eye. It only opened about halfway, but that was more than enough to show a dangerous glitter. "You call Olik a liar?" said the man – Olik.

"No," said Jim. He felt suddenly like doing one of those cartoon gulps, maybe even pulling at his collar with his forefinger. "No, not at all." He looked at the people in the other car. Normal early morning commuters. Coats, hats. Black, white, brown. Rich, poor. New Yorkers. "Just… wondering what's going on."

Olik's eye slowly closed. "Not important. Train goes to where we need. Is all that matters."

"Yeah, see?" Freddy stepped tentatively forward. "That's all that matters, right?"

As though they had been waiting for Freddy to do this, the doors slid shut. The train lurched forward. Freddy was caught off guard by the sudden motion and had to scramble to grab a support pole.

Adolfa, light and steady on her feet as a cat, sank back to her seat with a grin, clearly amused at Freddy's inability to stay upright. She winked at Jim.

Jim didn't feel like smiling. The day wasn't a laughing one. Not after the fight he'd had with Carolyn and Maddie.

Besides, the trains on this line usually had a piped-in announcement system that said when the train was going to leave, where it was headed, when it would probably get there. None of that had happened.

And the doors to the other cars *hadn't opened*? What was that about?

More than anything, though, something about the way the doors had slid shut behind Freddy unnerved Jim. The way they closed as soon as he was fully inside. Like they had been waiting to snap shut behind him. Like the train was a beast waiting to feed.

Like the people inside weren't passengers.

Like they were a meal.

THREE

The train pulled into the subway tunnel. Sound changed, the way it always did when the subway went into the darkness of the underground tube. As though the world outside had ceased to exist, or at the very least had lessened in reality, in force. They were traveling out of the world above and into a shadow-plane, a place that only joined the "real" at specified anchor points.

It was something Jim did all the time. But though it was something he should have been well-used to, he felt uneasy. Like today's trip was different.

The skull....

No. Not a skull. Just lights. Just a skinny man under some seriously bad lighting.

Jim looked around the car. Lawyer-lady was still texting. Olik the Russian scary guy was still somehow managing to look both asleep and simultaneously ready to pounce on the first person to bother him. The gangbanger was staring intently at nothing, his gaze as hard and featureless as a piece of dark slate.

And Freddy the Perv had ambled to the very back of the car, his hands thrust deep in the pockets of his trench coat and a new lollipop in his mouth.

"Who was in the picture?" said Adolfa.

It took a moment for Jim to realize that the old lady was talking to him. "Huh?" Then the words filtered through the fog that had seemed to lay over everything since the argument earlier that morning. "Oh, my girls." He looked to make sure that Freddy was out of earshot, then sat next to Adolfa. The hard plastic of the subway chair was cold. It felt like he was sitting on a piece of ice that instantly carved right through the layers of his coat, his pants. He shivered.

Jim checked once more to make sure that Freddy was far away, then pulled his journal out of his pants pocket. He flipped it open to the center, where he had tucked the picture, and held it out for Adolfa to see. "Carolyn," he said, pointing at the blonde beauty. His finger moved a bit, pointing now at the dark little girl in the blonde's arms. "And Maddison. Maddie."

Adolfa nodded as though she approved. "Lovely," she said.

Jim looked at the picture a moment longer before closing the journal around the photo and replacing both in his pocket. Part of him was aware how old-fashioned it was to actually carry around a wallet-portrait in the first place: in a world where everyone had their family pictures – family *pix* – on a phone or a tablet, he must look a bit like a dinosaur. But those electronic photos didn't have the same feel, the same *reality* that a wallet picture had. "Yeah," he said as he patted the rectangle bulge that carried the treasure. "Lovely." He smiled, but knew the smile was more regretful than he wanted it to be.

"What is it?" asked Adolfa.

Jim shook his head. "Nothing much. Just a bit of a fight."

Adolfa leaned back and smiled. She rubbed her legs, clearly still troubled by the aches she had complained of earlier. "I know about fights. Don't let it get old. New fights are okay, but if you let this fight get old...." She wiped imaginary sweat off her forehead, as though she had just done a job of tremendous difficulty. "Phew!"

"Noted."

They sat in silence for a moment. Jim hated this part. He didn't mind friendly people, and tried to be friendly himself. But he always felt awkward in the moments after the initial burst of camaraderie. Was he supposed to keep talking? Leave Adolfa alone? Did he start prattling, or just stay silent? Sometimes he felt like everyone else had been given a social instruction book but he'd somehow lost his. Like he was an alien in a world of humans, or vice-versa.

He had just decided to go ahead and leave the lady to her own devices – not the friendliest choice in the world, perhaps, but often the safest – when the lights went out.

This was not in itself unusual. Every New Yorker worth his or her salt had passed a moment or two in darkness on the subway. Lights sometimes flickered and flitted on and off like lightning bugs in a windstorm, as though someone had his hand on a huge On/Off switch and was constantly playing with the subway passengers; seeing what they would do if plunged into stroboscopic fits of light and dark. You got used to it. You ignored it.

What made *this* moment unusual was its duration and its momentum. Generally if the lights glitched on a subway, it only lasted for a second, a blink of the eyes when pitch darkness ruled. And if it was any longer than that the subway almost always slowed.

Neither rule held true in this situation. The lights stayed off far longer than a second or two. Jim couldn't be sure *how* long, but long enough that his heart started to beat hammer-blows against his ribcage, long enough that his breath started to come quick and shallow.

"What's going on?" said Freddy with his distinctive voice, that whine even higher now that panic was setting in. "What's happening?"

The train lurched, then the ever-present whine of the train's electric engine increased in volume. It sounded – *felt* – like the train was speeding up.

"What's going on?" Freddy again. The perv's voice, coming from the very back of the train, sounded like the voice of a person about to crack, about to plunge headfirst into a dark chasm of madness. Jim had a moment to wonder how close to that chasm Freddy had been *before* stepping onto the subway, if mere darkness could push him over that edge –

(*unless he knows something we don't*)

– before light speared through the car.

The light should have been comforting, should have been pleasing. It should have reminded Jim that he was okay, that he still had his girls to return to – fight or no fight – and that all was essentially right with the world.

But it did none of those things.

The light was cold and blue, providing no warmth or comfort but only a strange sense of *other*ness, as though the train had somehow been transported to an alternate dimension in its entirety. It came from the cell phone of the surly Olik. The big man was holding it above his head like a torch in a monster movie, moving it about as though the cell phone's sterile blue light might banish not only the darkness but the pervasive sense of strangeness that Jim could tell had gripped all the subway car's occupants.

"What is this?" said Olik. "What's going on?"

Beside Jim, Adolfa crossed herself.

Jim looked at the back of the car. Freddy was hunched against the rear bulkhead, quivering. He was slumped low, almost disappearing into his trench coat like some weird species of turtle that had evolved exclusively in cheap outlet malls. He looked terrified beyond reason.

Jim swiveled his head. Toward the front of the car, the gangbanger was looking back at the rest of the occupants, glaring as though one of them must be at fault for what was happening.

Only the beautiful lawyer-looking woman appeared unperturbed. Or at least, Jim thought she did at first; then he realized that the dark glint in her eyes wasn't just the cold reflection of Olik's cell-light. It wasn't fierceness or determination. It was terror, bound and caged like a feral beast held captive behind thick acrylic at a zoo. But the beast was pounding at the walls of its cage, beating at the boundaries of her eyes, struggling to be free. He abruptly felt like the lawyer might be the most dangerous person in the car. Which was ridiculous, he knew – he'd bet his life that Olik or the gangbanger held that dubious honor – but he couldn't deny the sudden sensation that the woman was someone not to be crossed under any circumstances.

Jim looked away from her. As much to pull his gaze from the too-riveting sight of her eyes and whatever mystery they held as to do an actual review of the subway car and the near-darkness in which they found themselves.

He looked beyond her. Beyond the lawyer. At the doors that led to the other cars. At the occupants in the car beyond this one.

And he screamed.

FOUR

Jim did not expect Olik's reaction to his scream. The gangbanger drew a knife, which wasn't surprising. The lawyer didn't move at all, which *was* surprising – he would have thought that she would have jumped at the very least, but the lawyer remained perfectly, completely still.

Adolfa drew a bit closer to him. Freddy yelped in tandem with Jim's scream. But Olik....

Olik pulled out a gun equipped with a silencer and squeezed off a pair of shots before Jim's scream had a chance to finish bouncing off the metal and plastic interior of the subway car. Nor were they panic-shots, randomly fired into the air or the floor: Jim saw two very closely grouped bullet holes in the glass window of the door dividing their car from the next.

"What the *hell*?" That was the gangbanger, though Jim heard the sentiment echoed in his own mind.

They were all cast into darkness again as Olik's cell phone – which he had held aloft even while shooting – suddenly switched off. The older man flipped it back on less than a second later. The blue-white light returned to the car, an illumination that did little to drive away shadows. Rather, it seemed only to point them out and highlight their existence. Jim was reminded of something his mother had said to him once. "Shadows only exist near to light," she had said.

And she had known more than a little about darkness. She had been murdered.

He turned his mind away from that. There was enough to think about right now without going there.

"What the hell do you think you're doing, man?" demanded the gangbanger. He approached Olik, seemingly unaware of the gun that the huge man still held. "You coulda killed me, man."

Olik ignored him. He turned to Jim. "You saw it, yes?"

"I...." Jim swallowed. His throat felt beyond dry. "I don't know what I saw."

"What did you see?" asked Adolfa. "What was it?" She was staring at him earnestly. He felt a hand on his wrist, a hand that curled around until it was holding onto his, and he drew strength from it. From her.

He shook his head, but found his voice. "I couldn't see much. Not in the dark. But it looked for a second like... like they were all dead."

"What?" The gangbanger's face became a caricature of incredulity. "What the hell you talkin', man?"

Freddy yelped again as Olik's cell-light flicked off. Black. *Pitch black.* Jim had heard those words before, but had never understood them. Pitch black wasn't a dark room, it wasn't a movie theater before the show started, it wasn't even the darkest places in a person's mind. Pitch black was a speeding subway deep under the city, all the lights out, and only strangers for company.

The blue-white light came on again. Then it was joined by another light, this one even brighter. Everyone looked over. It was the lawyer-type. She was holding a keychain light, one of those LED lamps that seemed to have around seven hundred bulbs on them and the same candle power as the Bat-signal. Olik nodded in thanks and put his cell phone back in his pocket.

Everyone turned back to Jim. The gangbanger jabbed his knife at him. Even in the light of a single keychain lamp, Jim could see that the knife was wickedly sharp, a six-inch blade with a razor edge that looked well-used and a handle that appeared supremely comfortable in the man's grip. No show knife, this was an instrument designed for – and accustomed to – the drawing of blood.

"What's this you talkin' about?" said the guy. "What's this everyone's dead shit?"

Jim shook his head. Suddenly the knife had become a much larger problem. The lawyer-type came to his defense. She pointed the LED lamp at the gangbanger so he had to raise a hand to shield his eyes. "Easy, buddy," she said. "You're scaring him."

"Put away that light, bitch, or I'll do more than scare *you*."

She ignored him, but swung the light back to a neutral position and asked, in calm and measured tones, "What did you see?"

Jim felt everyone's eyes on him. And suddenly didn't want to say what he had seen. Not again. He looked at Olik, as though to share the responsibility of what had happened, to dilute the reality of what *was* happening.

"You saw it, too, didn't you?" he said.

Olik pursed his thick lips. "I don't know what I see."

"But you shot them, man," said the gangbanger. He jabbed at Olik with his knife, the same gesture he had made at Jim. Apparently it was one of the primary ways he expressed himself, as though whenever he ran into an emotion too big for his mind to contain he stored part of it in that blade.

Olik, however, was not Jim. The blade didn't frighten him at all. It didn't even anger him. The older man's lip curled in irritation. "What is your name, little boy?" he asked.

"Little...?" The thug's eyes widened in disbelief at being addressed so patronizingly. He took a step toward Olik, and his knife was already thrusting forward. Then his movement – and that of his knife – utterly ceased as Olik's gun came up. Pointed squarely at the gangbanger's face. And Jim could see from the big man's expression that Olik would have no problem blowing the other man's brains out of the back of his head.

"Name, little boy." Olik cocked the gun.

The gangbanger's eyes got darker. Jim could see the thug calculating his chances of getting around the gun and gutting Olik. Apparently he decided discretion was the better part of valor. "Name's Xavier Gabriel."

Olik's eyes flickered. He chuckled. "I've heard of you, Mr. Gabriel."

"Then you know not to get in my way."

"Perhaps not in your hood." Olik smiled, then grew serious again. "But we're not in your hood, are we?"

Then, as suddenly as it had appeared, Olik's gun was gone. Jim didn't even see the man put it away, the older man moved so fast. He was dimly aware that holstering a silenced pistol must be even harder than putting away one without a sound suppressor, and he wondered what exactly Olik did for a living. Whatever it was, it seemed clear that Olik was a dangerous man. Still, with his weapon put away Jim wondered if Xavier was going to go ahead and eviscerate the older man now.

Apparently the rest of the car was wondering the same thing. The lawyer-type took a discrete step back, and Jim could see Freddy the Perv start shaking even harder. Only Adolfa seemed unworried, massaging her legs as she sat as though the main concern she had in all this was varicose veins and swollen ankles.

Xavier passed his knife from hand to hand. He was staring at Olik. The older man spread his arms wide, as though inviting the thug to attack.

"Come on," said Olik. "I let you take your best shot. But then you don't ever find out what Olik saw."

Xavier paused in his one-knife juggling act, curiosity clearly struggling with a desire to kill the man who had made him lose face. Curiosity finally won.

"What?" he said. "What you see?"

Olik laid a finger on the side of his nose. It was a quaint gesture, one that would have brought to mind Santa Claus or a kindly older uncle about to share a special secret, if it weren't for the expression on his face. Olik still looked like a slab of granite, but there were now veins of fear running through the rock of his expression.

"I saw the dead. The dead have come for us."

FIVE

Xavier's   expression

curled in on itself like a snake eating its own tail. His chin moved contemptuously in Jim's direction. "That's the same crack-smoking junk he said."

Olik smiled and shook his head. "No," he said. "The little man said he saw all the other passengers dead. *I* say I see the dead *come for us*. Is different."

The lights flickered on for a moment. Just a moment, enough for everyone to breathe a deep sigh of relief. Then they went out again, and all that was left was the glaring light of the lawyer's keychain. Jim glanced at Adolfa. The old woman was no longer kneading her legs. She had leaned back on her plastic subway seat, pressed so far back that she looked like she was trying to escape through the metal of the car siding. Her face, even in the white glare of the lawyer's key-light, was pale.

"You okay?" asked Jim.

She nodded, but he could tell she was nodding for herself as much as for him: sometimes we lie to others in the hope that what we say will become true to ourselves. Jim saw that kind of thing all the time. Sometimes it worked.

Xavier stepped forward. "I don't know what you fools are talking about," he said. "Ain't no dead people on this train."

He pointed his knife at Jim, who would have fallen back a step if he could have done so without landing either in Adolfa's lap or Olik's arms. "What did you see, 'zactly?"

Jim shook his head. "I don't know." Xavier's ever-excitable knife jumped forward. Jim's hands raised. "Easy, man. I really don't know! It looked – just for a second – like the people in the car were all dead."

"Dead how?" said the lawyer. Again, her voice was calm. Like she had found herself in this situation before and would undoubtedly do so again.

"Just dead. Slumped over."

"Asleep?" she said. Her voice was throaty. The kind of voice that a lot of men thought of as sexy.

Admit it, Jim, you think it's a sexy voice, too. It's not like you're cheating on Carolyn.

He forced his thoughts away from that.

Would you rather think about the fight? About the words that should never have been said?

That was worse, of course. So he answered, as much to keep from thinking about the fight as anything. "No, not like they were asleep. Their eyes were open. Staring." He shuddered.

Adolfa reached out and curled her hands around the crook of his elbow. He patted her bony knuckles and tossed an appreciative grin at her.

Xavier snorted. "So you saw a bunch of stiffs, and the Russki says he saw a bunch of zombies?"

"I never say zombies," said Olik. "I'm no peasant. And I'm Georgian. Not Russki."

"Whatever, Gramps." Xavier held out a hand to the lawyer.

She looked at his hand like she expected it to slither away from his arm and bite her. "What?" she said.

"The light, bitch. I'm gonna look at the next car."

She held the light away from him. Almost taunting. Jim wondered if the woman noticed the knife Xavier was holding, or if she was perhaps one of those special class of insane people who believe they are so important to the world that nothing can hurt them. Jim had met plenty of those in his life as well, and they all had one thing in common: they all bled as easily as anyone else.

"You're going to check the car?" she said. "You don't actually *believe* that there are dead people, do you?" She twirled the LED light in her hand, making shadows dance mad spirals in the car.

Jim could see that Xavier was about to crack. He edged back until he felt a row of plastic seats pressed against his legs. He noticed Olik's stance grow looser as well, as though the older man were preparing for mayhem. Everyone seemed to know the danger except the beautiful woman with the light.

"Listen, bitch —" began Xavier.

"Don't call me that," said the woman. Her voice slapped out, low but dangerous, reminiscent of the sound Olik's gun had made when he discharged it in the confines of the subway car. Then she smiled disarmingly. A genuine smile, full of warmth and perhaps just a hint of flirtation. "My name's Karen," she said, and then stepped past Xavier.

The move was so quick and graceful that the thug didn't have a chance to respond or do more than turn his head and track her with his eyes. She was ten feet from the front of the car before she turned back to him. "Coming?" she said, and actually batted her eyes coquettishly at him, as though this was all some kind of an elaborate prank for some basic cable show and she was the only person in on it.

Xavier's jaw clenched. Jim knew that Karen had to have seen it, had to have seen the deadly look in the gangster's eyes, but she just kept looking at him like she was waiting for a new beau to accompany her on a jaunt to the market. Finally, Xavier stepped forward. But he only took a few steps before he turned back and stared at Olik.

"What'd *you* see?"

"The dead, coming –"

"Yeah, yeah," said Xavier. He slashed the air with his knife. "That don't tell me shit, Grampa."

Olik crossed his arms across his barrel-chest. "I'm not a grandfather, *boy*."

Xavier looked like he was ready to start fighting at the word again, but Karen sighed. "When you two are done measuring your penises...." She jerked her head toward the front of the car. "This girl's getting like Alice in Wonderland up here."

"What's that mean?" Xavier demanded.

"Curiouser and curiouser," said Jim.

Karen nodded approvingly at him. "Someone's actually read a book."

Jim felt himself flush. "It's one of Maddie's favorites. My little girl," he said, aware that he was putting a wall between himself and the beautiful woman, also aware that doing so in such a purposeful and obvious way spoke volumes of how attracted he was to her. But it was the right thing to do.

Karen nodded again, and Jim suddenly had the strange impression that she could hear every thought in his head. He flushed; had to actively will himself not to look away from her.

"C'mon, cutie," Karen said to Xavier. The gangster smiled, a predatory expression reminiscent of the permanent grin of a great white shark. That was what the man was, too, Jim could tell. He was one of those hunters that endlessly circled the fringes of the city, one of those killers who understood that for them to rest was to die. Xavier's teeth were startlingly white against his dark skin, bright even in the darkness of the poorly-lit subway car. Not a warm smile, but the death-grin of a monster about to feed.

"Coming," he said, his voice suddenly and shockingly mellifluous.

That's what the spider sounds like in the instant it invites the fly to come on in, thought Jim. And he knew that Xavier had put his sights on Karen. Knew that the beautiful woman was as good as dead if the thug got half a chance.

But not now. Not when the two were in full view of the other people in the car. Xavier and Karen proceeded side by side like a force recon team, he holding his blade before him, she holding her light. They moved slowly, as though expecting something to explode out from below one of the plastic seats that lined the sides of the subway car.

Jim realized he was getting dizzy. He was holding his breath. He let it out, doing his best not to exhale too explosively. He breathed in again, and let himself sink down next to Adolfa. She curled her arm around his. He was glad for the contact, the comfort.

He looked at Olik. The man had his arms crossed, his face set like that of a statue. But he didn't look calm and composed the way he had when he first got onto the subway car. His expression before had been a *lack* of expression, a complete nothing. Now he looked like he was expending considerable energy *making* himself show nothing. And Jim knew that in itself showed much. Olik was frightened.

Jim moved his gaze beyond the Georgian. To Freddy the Perv, who hadn't moved from his crouch at the back of the subway. He was no longer trembling, no longer shaking. But he still looked terrified. He had finished his lollipop and was just working the stick around in his mouth until it had become a white, flattened mess. He licked his lips around the stick, and the gesture made Jim feel ill.

"Dammit."

Jim looked back to the front of the car. Xavier and Karen were at the door that separated this car from the next one, shining Karen's light at the glass. From where Jim sat, it looked like the glass has been painted black. That was impossible, of course: it *seemed* like much longer, but in reality only a few short moments had passed between his glimpsing what looked like a cabin full of dead people in the next car and this moment. Certainly it had been too short a time for someone to steal into the subway car and paint the glass between the cars black, even if such could have been done without them noticing it.

Still, he couldn't deny that *was* what it looked like. He could even see an almost-perfect reflection of Karen's flashlight in the glass, bouncing toward the back of the car as she angled it now this way, now that in an attempt to see what lay beyond the window. Both she and Xavier were moving around as well, the way a person does when trying to see through a screen door into a dimly-lit room in the middle of a bright summer day.

"Well?" called out Olik. His voice was flat. As though he didn't really expect them to see anything.

Xavier glared back at them. The way Karen's light bounced off the glass behind his face backlit him eerily, creating a strange skull of his features. The tattoos that curled up around his neck took on the appearance of mystical runes, curling snakes of dark magic. The tear-tattoos made him seem like a voodoo priest, weeping blood sacrifices for a dark god of death.

Then Xavier turned back to the door. There was a handle on the door, a handle that every New Yorker knew was for opening the door and moving car to car – just as every New Yorker knew it was illegal to do so. Indeed, there were several signs posted on and around the door warning of the illegality of moving between the subway cars while the train was in motion.

Xavier pushed at it, then pulled at it. He yanked and scuffled with it. Then he abandoned the handle and simply settled for slamming his shoulder into the door itself. The entire car swayed with the force of the blows, but no matter how hard the man hit it, the steel door itself didn't move.

"What do you see?" said Olik.

"Nothing," said Karen. She let her light point down at the same time, as though admitting defeat both vocally and physically. She eyed Xavier. "Easy, slugger."

Xavier slammed into the door one more time, then stopped. He punched the door beside the glass. "Won't open," he said. "The doors are *always* supposed to open." He hit the door again. "That's against the law."

"It's against the law to open it while the train's moving, too," said Karen, pointing at the signs.

Xavier rolled his eyes. He gave the handle a last jiggle. Jim noted that the gangster's knife had somehow disappeared into his coat. Like Olik, the gangster apparently belonged to a group of magicians who could make weapons disappear at will.

His thoughts were cut off when Karen came back toward them. Xavier followed her. Jim knew the thug would have denied it, but he strongly suspected that he didn't want to be too far away from the light.

"There was nothing," said Karen.

"What you mean, nothing?" said Olik.

"I mean nothing nothing," said Karen. "Just black. Like we were in a hole."

"That's impossible." Freddy the Perv spoke up for the first time, his voice high and jittering, putting Jim on edge faster than the sound of a dentist's drill on enamel. He stepped toward the group. "There's gotta be *something*."

"You callin' her a liar?" said Xavier.

Freddy shrank back into the shadows in the rear of the car. "Nah," he said. His voice fell off to a whisper. "If you say there's nothing, then that's what there is."

"It's like someone covered the window," said Karen. "Nothing but black."

Olik looked at Xavier for confirmation. Xavier nodded. "True. Can't see shit."

"Nobody covered over window," said Olik.

"Not saying someone *did*," said Xavier. "Just saying that's what it *looks* like." He rubbed at his shoulder. "And I couldn't get through the door, either."

Olik grinned tightly. He had the same shark-grin as Xavier, Jim saw. He reached into his coat. "I have key to any door," he said, and withdrew his gun.

"It will not work, my Georgian friend," said Adolfa.

Olik looked at the old woman in surprise, and even Jim was a bit startled. Adolfa had been so quiet that he had almost forgotten she was there. But Olik's smile quickly returned. "Not many locks stand against this key," he said.

"I don't doubt it," she said. "But this one already has."

"What you mean?" said Olik.

"You shot twice," she said. "Two very good shots, nice and tight, through the window."

"Yes?" Olik's face scarcely moved. It remained a solid slab of white, with only a few wrinkles around his eyes betraying his confusion.

Adolfa waved toward the front of the train. "The window is black, yes?"

"Yeah," said Xavier.

"So this is not a question. The window is black, and that is fact," said Adolfa. "But what *is* a question is this: where did the bullet holes go?"

Karen swung her LED over, and everyone looked where she pointed it. None of them had noticed – none but Adolfa – but Jim saw she was right.

Olik had squeezed off two shots. Tightly grouped, expertly placed. Two slugs right through the glass window separating the cars.

The window that had been transparent but was now dark.

The window that had held two circles where the bullets had passed through it...

... but was now, inexplicably – impossibly – whole.

SIX

Olik laughed. It was one of the least-jolly sounds that Jim could ever remember hearing. Almost as cold as –

(the sound of the first hit, the argument just beginning and already we were fighting, already she was resorting to physical abuse)

– the *whft* of the suppressor as Olik fired another pair of shots through the window. Again they appeared as by magic, twin circles with snow-crackled edges illuminated by the swaying light Karen still held in the speeding subway car.

"There," said Olik. Karen's light swung back to the older man, illuminating his face as he kissed the handle of his gun. As he did so, Olik's coat opened enough that Jim could see a shoulder holster that held another gun, the twin of the one the Georgian man held.

Geez, thought Jim, who *is* this guy?

Then he felt Adolfa's arm, which had once again curled into the crook of his own, tighten. She hissed. It was a strange sound, one that he had never heard a grown woman make before but which he nonetheless instantly understood.

Danger, the noise said.

43

The others must have heard the same warning in the sound. Karen swung her light toward the old lady, but Adolfa waved the spear-beam away, pointing a crooked finger toward the front of the car.

Karen pointed her light at the door. The window.

"Your key did not work," said Adolfa.

Olik said something in Georgian, something short and sharp that sounded like it was nothing but consonants and could only be a prayer or a curse.

The window was whole again.

"Gotta be a trick of the light," said Xavier.

"Is no trick," said Olik. His face was whiter than ever, almost glowing in the dark car. "No trick."

"Bull," said Xavier. He walked forward.

Karen reached out and grabbed his coated arm when he passed her. "Don't," she said.

Xavier smiled, now looking more like a wolf than a shark. Something more inclined to mate before it fed. "Didn't know you cared," he said.

"You don't know what's there," Karen said.

"Never will if we don't check it out," he said. He shook free of her almost contemptuously.

Karen shook her head. Not angry, just resigned, like she was watching a rookie make a bad move in a ball game. "Smart money says just wait until we reach the next stop and figure it out then."

Xavier looked back at her, and this time there was no mistaking the contempt in his gaze. "Bitch, ain't gonna *be* a next stop." He pulled back his coat sleeve and showed her a watch. "Shoulda hit the 'next stop' ten minutes ago."

He moved forward again. "Don't know where we're goin', but wherever it is, it ain't on the transit maps."

SEVEN

Jim did the same thing everyone else did: he checked his cell phone. No one – except Xavier – even had a watch anymore. Not even Adolfa, who seemed like the kind of person who might wear an old-fashioned wind-up, was wearing a timepiece. Just a variety of smartphones and flip-phones that had replaced single-function watches.

It took less than a second to verify what Xavier had said, then another second to glance up at the plastic boards bolted to the subway car here and there that stated what route this was. It wasn't an express, which meant they *should* have pulled in to their next stop by now.

Karen hummed a quick ditty under her breath that Jim realized was the theme to the old *Twilight Zone* show. For a moment he thought she was right, then he realized it was unlikely they had found themselves in anything as benign as Rod Serling's classic of strangeness. No, what was happening now was infinitely more bizarre, infinitely more… threatening.

Up front, Xavier was closing in on the door between subway cars, with its once-more-unmarred window. Karen had aimed her light at him, but with the rock of the subway car it was dancing around so much Xavier almost seemed like a ghost, flitting back and forth far too much with every movement he made. At first Jim thought the train must be speeding up, then he realized that Karen was scared. Her hand was shaking.

He looked at his cell phone. Stared at it dumbly for a moment, then laughed. The sound was over-bright, an unwelcome intruder in the darkness. He felt everyone's eyes on him. Even Xavier swiveled to face him, with an angry "What the –?" harsh on his lips.

Jim waved his phone. "The phones," he laughed.

"What?" Olik said.

"We can *call* someone," said Jim. Olik, Karen, and Xavier just stared at him like he had suddenly sprouted a second head – one that said exclusively stupid things. Only Adolfa seemed willing even to entertain the idea that something as simple as a phone call could get them out of this.

"Go ahead," she said.

But all of a sudden, Jim didn't want to be the one who called anyone. Didn't want to be the one who bore that responsibility. Plus –

(*plus who would he call?*)

– he had to admit to a suspicion, now that his thumb hovered over the dial numerals, that this *wouldn't* work. After all, if someone could purloin an entire subway train en route and then replace a bullet-riddled window not once but twice, who was he to think that a mere phone call would get them out of... whatever this was?

"You call," he said, and pushed his phone over to Adolfa.

The old lady looked askance at him, clearly unsure why he didn't make the call himself, but she took the phone. She seemed to consider a moment, then simply dialed "911" before pressing the "SEND" button.

Jim could feel the others in the train car, holding their breaths as one, looking at Adolfa as though she held their futures in her hand. Perhaps she did.

She put the phone to her ear. Listened. Frowned.

"Nothing," she said. "No bars."

"Not surprising," said Karen. "We're under a couple of hundred feet of steel and concrete, after all. Hardly the best place for cell reception."

"Not on this line," said Freddy.

"Shut up, man," said Xavier. Jim could tell that the thug felt the same instant revulsion at the mere sound of Freddy's voice that Jim did, and suddenly felt a strange kinship with the man.

"Let him talk," said Olik, and gestured Freddy forward.

The mousy man looked unsure, as though he didn't know whether he'd prefer to piss off Olik or Xavier, but finally he scampered toward the middle of the car. "This line has boosters," he said. "It's supposed to get cell reception."

"Bullshit," said Xavier.

Jim shook his head. "Boosters are for wifi, not for cell reception," he said.

Freddy's expression fell, but only for a moment. "So somebody got a tablet or a laptop?" he said.

Jim looked around. Finally Karen said, "I do," in a tone of voice that indicated she would almost rather be torn to bits by wild dogs than follow along with a scheme proposed by Freddy. Still she walked to where she had been sitting earlier, to the spot where her leather satchel still rested.

She opened it. Jim was a bit surprised that she had left it alone in the middle of the aisle in the first place, then realized she probably wasn't worried about anyone stealing it: where would they go? And there were only seven people total in the car, so if her bag did disappear, figuring out who took it wouldn't be too hard.

Plus, he noted, the bag had a pair of subtle but sturdy-looking combination locks.

Karen unlocked her bag and pulled out a small tablet computer. She shut and locked the bag again, then returned to the group. She pressed the power button and the tablet screen illuminated, showing a lock-screen. The woman keyed in four numbers.

The screen went black, then turned to a blue screen with a pair of icons: one for a web browser and one for a webmail program.

Not the most personable homescreen, thought Jim. The girl's definitely a midtown lawyer.

"What now?" said Karen.

"NYPD has an online request form," said Freddy. Jim had to repress a shudder, because he suspected that the other man was a frequent reader of such request forms – probably as the subject of requests that the cops do something to keep him away from the neighborhood kids.

"So what do you want me to request?" said Karen with a smirk. But she touched the web browser icon.

"How about you request that they get us the hell off this train?" said Xavier.

"Good start," said Olik.

The tablet flickered. The web browser came on, and for a single moment Jim saw the familiar pattern of Google's search screen on the page.

"Nice. Home free," breathed Freddy.

Then the Google search screen disappeared. In its place, a face came into view. The face was bloated, swollen. The tongue protruded grossly, the individual taste buds visible even on the tablet's small screen. The eyes were rolled back, the scleras grey and bulging from the eye sockets.

Adolfa gasped beside Jim. She crossed herself.

The face disappeared. Another one flashed into view. This one was of a woman, her eyes looking up and in, rendering her slightly cross-eyed as though she were seeking to look at the ragged bullet-wound that had perforated her forehead.

Then that face, too, was gone. Another came. And another, and another, and another. All of them were the faces of the dead, clearly victims of foul play. Gunshot wounds, knife wounds, loops and lassoes tied around necks, noses cut off and tongues cut out. Faster and faster they came, each image more gruesome than the last until they started to melt into each other. They became a single waxy entity, a thing that had fused into a nightmare essence of every kind of violence imaginable.

The many-faced thing's mouth moved. The tongue had been hacked out at the roots, it had been cut in two, it had been yanked out with pliers, it had been grated off with a belt-sander. Jim knew all this just by looking at it, and knew that the others knew it as well – though he couldn't say how he knew either of these things.

In spite of the fact that the thing – the *things*, the *legion* – was possessed either of no tongue or of a tongue that had been rent and torn a thousand times over, the face on Karen's tablet spoke. It spoke, and as it did its dead eyes opened. They roved over the assembled travelers, and Jim knew that they were looking at each person in turn.

"Murderer," the voice whispered. The voice of the dead, bloody and torn and abused until its last breath was yanked from its lungs, until its will to live was crushed and destroyed and drowned in a tidal wave of blood.

And now blood spilled from the thing's mouth. "Murderer," it said again. The words burbled and drowned in the fluid.

Karen screamed, and Jim realized with a start that the blood wasn't just coming from the mouth of the death-thing on the screen; it was coming from the screen *itself*. Dark red fluid cascaded down the tablet screen like a bloody waterfall.

The blood touched Karen's hands, covering them in an instant. It ran over her fingers, and her hands and arms ran red with blood. She screamed again, and this time she dropped the tablet.

The small computer fell with a clatter to the steel floor of the subway car. It fell face-down, the images disappearing for a merciful moment. Then, though Jim was sure the tablet had come completely and utterly to rest – there was no remaining kinetic energy in the small computer – the tablet flipped itself over as though some unknown hand had turned it face up.

The death-thing still looked at them. Its face still waxed and shifted from one maimed visage to another.

A man, eyes put out by metal spikes….

A woman, throat cut ear to ear….

Another man, face all but obliterated by what Jim guessed must be a shotgun blast at point-blank range….

And then a *child*. Young. Too young to contemplate, too young to believe. But there he was. Or perhaps she. The face was so young that it could as easily be a boy as it was a girl. And it was clearly dead as the others. Dead, eyes yellowed and lips blue and cheeks pale and waxy.

Beside Jim, Adolfa sobbed. Xavier cursed nearby.

"You killed me," said the child in a voice that was almost surprised. Its face began to melt. Not into another face, another horrid caricature of death, but like a candle losing its shape. Before all structure was gone, though, the child/creature/thing opened its sagging mouth and let loose a shriek. The sound was terrible, too loud to come from the tiny speakers built into the tablet. So loud that Jim felt like his ears might explode.

He clapped his hands over his ears. Beside him, Adolfa did the same. So did Karen. Xavier. Freddy. Finally Olik did, too.

There was a popping sound. Darkness reached heavy fingers farther into the subway car. Jim couldn't figure out what had happened for a moment, then realized that Karen's LED lamp had burst. The scream from the child on the tablet had destroyed her light.

How is that possible? How is that possible? What's going on, what's happening and how is it possible?

Jim suddenly realized he was screaming, but he couldn't hear the sound of his own voice. He was shrieking deaf pleas to no one and nothing. Mute before the banshee wail of anger and betrayal coming from the floor of the subway car.

More popping sounds. Olik cursed. A moment later Jim felt something bite his leg. He realized what it was even in his pain: his phone, the screen shattering and sending shards through his pants leg. Nothing major, but his phone was shot. Probably Olik's, too. Probably everyone's phones were shot. Gone. They were on their own.

With a final rising peal, the child's shriek rose to a level beyond any that Jim thought he could stand.

I'm going to pass out.

But he didn't pass out. Not quite. Sparkling blobs of tinsel and globes like Christmas ornaments began jumping in front of his eyes, but before he blacked out completely something that sounded like a small explosion cracked through the subway car.

It was the tablet. The face of the undead child-thing screaming. The glass face of the tablet shattered and there was a single, searing flash of white light.

Then all was silent.

All was dark.

EIGHT

Jim didn't know how long they remained in darkness. It could have been a second, it could have been an hour. Time suddenly seemed mutable. Minutes interchangeable with years. Millennia could be mistaken for microseconds.

Is this what madness feels like?

He suspected it was. He suspected that here, floating in absolute darkness on a train that was careening towards God-only-knew where, madness was not an arm's length away from him as it was for so many of the people who walked the surface of a sometimes horrific world. No, here it was a companion, a bosom friend, a soul mate.

A soul mate.

Then something flashed, so bright it momentarily made him forget what he had just seen on Karen's tablet. The light cast him back into memory: the glint of lightning bugs in the forest. Running through the trees, the forested area that served as his backyard after finding his mother's body. Her murdered corpse, stabbed so many times the doctors later told him that they couldn't count the wounds.

Lightning bugs.

He blinked. It would be so easy, he realized, so easy to lose himself in the madness that reached out for him. So easy to let himself go and thereby give himself permission to just forget about figuring out what was happening right now.

Just give up.

Then he saw Carolyn's face. Maddie's. His girls.

The light came again. Not lightning bugs. He wasn't in that faraway forest, that long-ago place. He was in the train. The subway. Adolfa was holding onto him in the dark, he could hear her mumbling a prayer in Spanish, hushed tones that somehow spoke warmth to him.

The light flashed. It was coming from outside the subway car. And it was something so unexpectedly normal that he almost didn't recognize it. Xavier had pointed out that the train had somehow left its course, had somehow gone from a local train to an express route that went straight to some unknown destination, no stops, no new passengers. And with that change in service had come a blank darkness outside the train. Were it not for the click-clack of the wheels on the rails and the steady electrical hum of the motor, they could as well have been traveling through the vacuum of deep space or the even blanker nothing of a black hole.

But now... lights. And they were the lights that typically flashed by whenever the train passed through a subway tunnel. Jim didn't know what they were called, exactly, but he assumed they were there as some kind of safety or maintenance lights. Red, yellow, green, white.

And as soon as he recognized them, the lights came on in the car as well. The darkness dissipated. As though by finding a tiny piece of order, more order was called forth.

Jim looked around. Adolfa was sitting with him, but other than that everyone else had spread out in the darkness. It looked as though they were a group of sworn enemies, terrified that each would try some kind of mischief under cover of the black that had just enveloped them. Then he realized it wasn't that his fellow-passengers were concerned about each other: they were afraid of the tablet. Still sitting in the center of the train, its face shattered with the force of the shriek that had issued forth from its electronic circuitry – and from a place impossibly deeper and darker than that.

The others were looking around now. Karen held her shaking hands in front of her face. The blood that had flowed out of the tablet had stained her expensive coat and shirtsleeves almost black, and the wrinkles of her knuckles and palms were caked with coagulating gore. She shuddered and began rubbing her hands against each other, but no matter how hard she rubbed, it seemed like the red wouldn't come off.

She began to sob.

Xavier sat beyond her, at the front of the car. He had wedged himself halfway under one of the seats, his knife out in front of him like he expected to be attacked at any moment.

We are *being attacked. But by what?*

The large black man shook himself. He stood suddenly, as though by moving quickly he might throw off whatever spell had cast itself around the group. Then he strode past Karen, to the tablet. He fell on one knee beside it and began stabbing it with the knife.

56

Xavier didn't go crazy. He didn't start stabbing it maniacally, like an axe-murderer from some bad horror movie. He was methodical, his arm rising and falling with the perfect time of an expensive metronome. *Clack. Clack. Clack.* And the pure emotionless quality of his actions was more frightening than any crazed acting out would have been. Jim could see that he wasn't insane, he was just killing what he perceived as the only thing *to* be killed. For now.

Adolfa shifted. The movement must have caught Xavier's eye, because the man glanced at her. The look, the dead, empty look in his eyes, was terrifying. Adolfa immediately stiffened. Jim didn't move, either. He thought it likely that anyone Xavier perceived as a threat in the next few moments would probably end up as thoroughly mangled as Karen's tablet.

And indeed, a few seconds later there was almost nothing left of the electronic equipment. Just a few bits of plastic and glass on the metal floor of the car. Olik, who like everyone else had been watching Xavier without moving or speaking, finally stepped forward. He smiled a grim, almost angry smile. "You feel better?" he asked, and placed a thick hand on the gangbanger's shoulder.

Xavier nodded. Jewels of sweat had appeared on his neck and forehead, and more had dampened his knit cap. "Just wanted whoever's doing this to know what I'm gonna do to them when I find 'em."

Xavier clapped the man on the shoulder. "Good. Good fight in you," he said in his heavy, deep voice. "I heard that of you, too."

"We're going to die here," said Karen.

Everyone spun to look at her. She was still rubbing her hands on her clothes, the seat beside her, the metal poles nearby – anything she could use to create friction to burn off some of the blood that coated her skin. Jim thought it looked like she was sitting in the middle of a strangely-shaped butcher's block: everything crimson and stained, a place of death and killing.

Karen held her hands up. They were as red as ever. "It won't come off," she whispered. Then she shook her head and repeated, "We're going to die here."

Olik snorted. Xavier was more direct. "Speak for yourself, bitch."

Karen erupted forward, running at Xavier and plowing into him. *"DON'T CALL ME THAT!"* she shrieked. Jim didn't think the woman could have weighed more than one hundred twenty pounds – probably only about half of what the gangbanger clocked in at. So he would have expected her to just bounce off the thug. But instead the two of them went down in a pile. Xavier *oof*'d as the air rushed out of him, and Karen cocked a very un-lawyerly fist, clearly intent on doing her best to pound some manners into the guy.

Xavier was still holding his knife. Jim saw the man's hand tighten on the grip, knew that Karen was about to come to a very messy end. Maybe she'd be able to get a single punch in, but that was going to be it.

Olik moved. One huge foot stepped on Xavier's arm, pinning his knife hand to the floor of the train. At the same time, he plucked Karen up by the collar with no visible effort. She looked like an errant puppy in his huge hands.

"Stop, both of you," he growled.

"Let me up, motherf –" began Xavier. The vituperation became a choked-off scream as Olik ground his boot down. Then, turning to Karen, he punched her viciously in the face. There was a distinctive crack as her nose crumpled beneath his fist. Blood spurted. Karen flew back under the power of the blow. She hit one of the upright aluminum support bars, slingshotting around it and landing in a heap on the floor just beyond.

Jim was agape. He had a moment to wonder again who Olik was. Then the Georgian spoke. "Don't do this," he growled. "Don't attack each other. Problem isn't here," he said, gesturing at the passengers. "Problem is whoever is doing this." He glared at Xavier. "Don't make trouble in here."

"She hit me!" said Xavier. Jim was surprised how much the thug sounded like a peeved toddler in that moment.

Olik nodded. "And I punished her for this," he said. He shook a huge fist at Xavier. "Don't make me do same to you." Xavier glared, but finally nodded. "Besides...." Olik leaned in and whispered something in Xavier's ear. Xavier started, then looked at Karen, who was getting slowly to her feet, holding her blood-crusted hands to her spurting nose.

"What?" said Xavier. He sounded shocked. He looked at Olik with a strange light in his eyes. Admiration? Jim couldn't be sure, but he thought so.

Olik just nodded, then turned to everyone. "We need to put our heads together, yes? To think. Not to be enemies now."

"What's doing this?" asked Karen. She gave up holding her hands under her nose and just let the blood flow. Jim noted that even with a severely broken nose she still put most women's looks to shame. Some very good genetics at work there.

"That's what we figure out first," said Olik with an approving nod. "But we don't do it fighting, yes? We do it talking. We look around." He tapped his temple with a huge finger. "We use this."

Adolfa laughed. Jim looked at her with a mixture of dismay and admiration. The laugh hadn't been a mirthful one, but one of dismissal. "Strange words from a man who shoots so quickly," she said.

Olik looked as though he was trying to decide whether to be angry with her. Then he smiled ruefully and shrugged. "Everyone entitled to shoot when he sees the dead coming, yes?" he said. "Besides. Gun is away." He looked around the train car. It was rocking, *click-clack-click-clack-click-clack*. Lights still flashing outside the windows. Still moving, still going somewhere.

But where? Jim wondered. And how long would it take to get there?

"I think we have time," said Olik. "Time to think."

"Why you say that, man?" said Xavier. He got up as well, sitting on one of the plastic seats across from Jim. His knife was gone again, disappeared to whatever alternate universe location the gangbanger hid his weapons. Jim wondered what other armaments the guy might have on his person. Olik, too: just the two guns, or did he have more? A few knives, perhaps, or a grenade or two? Maybe an ankle-holster with a portable nuke?

"I say we have time because we are still safe," said Olik. He gestured around the car. "We are stuck here, but whatever is happening, it is to scare, not to kill, yes?"

Jim nodded.

Karen held up her hands. "What about this?"

"Not killing," said Olik. "You are still alive. Still alive, so still we can survive. Still we can escape this, whatever it is. Where there is life, there is hope, yes?"

Olik smiled. Karen smiled back, which was a surprise, Jim thought, considering that the Georgian had just cracked her nose like a walnut less than a minute ago. But at the same time, Jim felt like smiling, too. Because Olik was making some sense. They *weren't* dead, they weren't even hurt. Not really. Just trapped and scared.

So they could make it through whatever was happening.

They *would* make it.

Adolfa patted Jim, and he understood that she wasn't just trying to buoy him up, she was also saying that she felt better, too. That Olik's words had given her hope. Given them all hope. Even Xavier was smiling. It was a real smile, too. Not the smile of a predator contemplating which piece of its still-living prey to bite, but the smile of someone who believes he will survive to see another day.

Jim felt a smile cross his own face, as well.

And then the screaming started.

NINE

Freddy the Perv was the one making the noise. Jim had completely – blessedly – forgotten the man was even on the subway, hunched as he was in the back of the car like a dog that feared a beating. And from the looks Jim glimpsed on the others' faces, he could tell they had done the same.

But they weren't going to forget him again. Not if they lived to be a million years old.

Freddy was shouting, screaming, *shrieking*. A sound almost as loud and insistently horrifying as the one that had come out of the montage of corpses on Karen's tablet. Even worse, in a way, because the noise that had come from the electronic device had been one of rage and hate. And it hadn't been one of *them*. One of the six passengers in the car.

This noise, though, the sound that was coming out of Freddy's mouth in a sustained, high-pitched whistle, was one of pure, unfiltered pain. And it was definitely pain that had come to scratch out a home, a dark den, among *their* number.

"What? What's happening?" shouted Xavier. Freddy didn't answer, and the thug took a step toward him. "You better shut your face, man, or I'll shut it for –"

Then Xavier stopped moving. Stopped like he'd been paralyzed, like he'd been trapped in some sort of force field. If it weren't for the subtle rock of his body on the train, Jim could almost have believed he was looking at a wax statue of incredibly lifelike craftsmanship.

Jim looked back at Freddy, and he saw why the man was screaming so loudly. Saw also why Xavier had stopped moving toward the trench-coated man.

Freddy had his hands up in front of his face. Normal skin tones, though they looked somewhat sickly in the flickering fluorescent light of the subway car. His fingers were moving. Not bending at the knuckles, not knotting into fists. They weren't moving in any way that Jim had ever seen fingers move, in fact. They were almost *writhing*, he finally realized with a start. The thumbs, too. Like the digits were ten snakes that had awakened to find themselves attached at the base to some horrid tumor, and were now trying to escape from it.

At first Jim thought Freddy's fingers looked almost boneless. Then he realized how wrong that was. They didn't look boneless at all. Indeed, that was why Freddy was screaming so loud: underneath the sound of the scream, Jim could hear pin-crackles, a series of crunches so tiny and dampened they were almost delicate.

Freddy's fingers weren't simply moving, they were being *twisted*. Wrung like rags between strong hands, and the bones inside them had to be turning to splinters, then honeycombs, then jelly.

There was a moment of blessed, terrible silence as Freddy stopped screaming. He panted, breaths coming in staccato bursts that made Jim think of the needle on a sewing machine, dancing up and down. But instead of making pillows or quilts or comfy bits of homey goodness, this would have to be a sewing machine of the variety that Ed Gein would have used, a needle for stitching lengths of skin into macabre creations intended only for the enjoyment of the damned.

Freddy inhaled deeply, a clear precursor to another scream.

Xavier cursed.

Adolfa crossed herself.

Karen did not speak, but Jim saw her eyes alight with horror.

Only Olik seemed impassive.

Then there was another crunch, this one louder than the others had been. Freddy's impending scream was stolen from his lungs, streaming out in an exhalation of pain so intense it could be seen in every clenched muscle of his body.

His fingers – all of them – suddenly bent back on themselves. Bent double, like an unseen muscle-man had folded them backwards, folded them in half as easily as Jim might fold a soda can. The tortured skin of Freddy's fingers finally gave way, breaking at the unnatural corners that had just appeared. Freddy's flesh ruptured, bursting like the stomachs of so many over-gorged mosquitos, and a fine spray of blood flew into the air. It aerosolized almost immediately, a cloud of red that first dispersed and then disappeared.

Adolfa started to chant under her breath. Jim didn't speak more than a few words of Spanish – the tenacious holdovers from his school days – but he could tell it was a prayer.

"*Padre nuestro, que estás en el cielo,*" she said.

Popping sounds came from Freddy's fingers. It couldn't be bones, a strangely detached part of Jim's mind reasoned. They had to be Jell-O by now. The pops had to be the tendons giving way.

Karen retched.

Freddy inhaled again. Another attempt to scream. Again, he failed to finish the action.

"*Santificado sea tu nombre. Venga tu reino.*"

The perv's fingers snapped straight again, like they had been yanked forward. He exhaled, a shuddering breath that would have sounded almost orgasmic in other circumstances. But the expression on his face allowed only one interpretation: Freddy was in the grips of utmost agony.

"*Hágase tu voluntad en la tierra como en el cielo.*"

A horrible odor suddenly pervaded the subway car. Metallic and acrid, Jim had never smelled anything like it. His mind coughed up an image of car batteries cooking in an industrial oven, though he had no idea why he would think of that.

"*Danos hoy nustro pan de cada día.*"

A hissing sound joined the terrible stench that had suffused the car. Everyone looked around. Jim did, too, though he already knew where the sound was coming from. He suspected the others probably did, too. Perhaps they, like him, just didn't want to see, to *know*, any more.

But they did look. They had to. He knew that. They all knew that. They had to look. To see what was happening. Because it might happen to any of them next. So they had to see, in order to survive.

If that was even possible.

"Perdona nuestras ofensas..."

Freddy's fingers. No longer bent. But no longer straight, either. They sagged like putty, and then began to hiss and spit. They grew black and charred, and the skin sloughed off in flakes and then in sheets that left raw red meat beneath. This was the source of the smell, the smell of batteries cooking in an oven, of flesh melting in the heat of the sun.

"... como también nosotros perdonamos a los que nos ofenden."

Then the meat bubbled and blackened as well. It frothed like an oily surf washing up to a polluted shore. And when the froth fizzed away, Freddy's fingers were...

"No nos dejes caer en tentación..."

... gone.

"... y líbranos del mal."

Freddy looked at his hands, at the ten cauterized nubs where fingers had once been. And finally, finally, he managed to do what he had been attempting through the last moments.

Freddy the Perv screamed. And screamed and screamed and did not stop.

Adolfa crossed herself. She kissed her own still-present fingers.

"Amen."

TEN

"What's going on? What the *hell's* going on?" Xavier spat the words like bullets, as though convinced that if he spoke with enough vehemence or vitriol then the words themselves might force whoever was doing all this to reveal themselves and release their captive passengers.

Adolfa had a grip on Jim's arm again, and her other hand was clutching her blouse above her bosom. He wondered if she was having a heart attack; wondered what he would do if she *was* having a heart attack. It wasn't like he could perform CPR and wait for the paramedics to show up.

Freddy had stopped screaming. He was wheezing in the back of the car, looking at the blood-black stumps where his fingers had been, tears of pain and disbelief pouring down his cheeks. Olik stepped close to the wounded man, his pale face cocked to one side in a way Jim thought looked almost like absent curiosity. Which was insane. The Georgian should have been scared out of his mind, shouldn't he? Because whatever had just happened was enough to scare *anyone* out of his or her mind – anyone who had a mind to begin with, at least.

Unless he's *the one doing it.*

The thought came quite surprisingly, but there was a certain kind of appeal to it. Jim glanced at the huge man, who now had his head tilted to the other side, as though to get a different view of the suffering man in the back of the subway car.

Certainly Olik was the only one who had seemed to take everything that came in stride. Had seemed unfazed throughout... whatever was happening.

He was the one who shot the window.

Jim looked at the window in the door at the front of the car. Though the side windows had become transparent again, allowing the lights outside to be seen, the window at the front of the car was still black as pitch, as paint. Dark as the blackest part of space. He wondered if they *did* manage to force the door open, if they would get into the next subway car, or if it would just open into a void, into a blank nothing where existence had no meaning.

Focus, Jim. Concentrate on the problem.

He looked back at Olik. The Georgian hadn't moved. And apparently Jim wasn't the only one who had noticed the big man's imperturbability. Because at that moment Xavier moved forward, his now-you-see-it-now-you-don't knife visible once more.

"You did this, man," said the gangbanger.

Olik half-turned, as though whatever might be happening was less interesting than the fantastic view of Freddy the Miraculous Melting Man. "What?" he said.

"You heard me," snarled Xavier. "Hey, man, *look at me when I talk to you.*"

Jim, still seated beside Adolfa, pulled his feet out of the way as Xavier walked past. So did the *latina*, though she was small enough he suspected she could have stretched out full-length in the center aisle and not posed any kind of stumbling danger. But he understood the impulse: the look on the thug's face was more than just dangerous. There was murder there, pure and simple. He glanced down the car at Karen. The lawyer had picked up her satchel and was holding it tightly in her blood-stained hands, like a security blanket that might protect her from the nightmare that all of them had found themselves contained within.

Olik turned to look at Xavier. Not quickly, not in a panic, not even with any particular excitement that Jim could see. But there was still a noticeable increase in the tension in the car.

Please, God, let me get through this. Let me get back to Carolyn and Maddie.

"Okay, friend. I'm looking at you," said Olik. His voice – normally booming and authoritative, was quiet. And that scared Jim, too.

"You doing this, man?" said Xavier. He kept advancing on Olik. "You doing this shit? Because this shit is scaring me, it's scaring..." and he motioned at everyone else with his knife, "... alla them." Now he pointed the knife at Olik. "But it ain't scaring you."

Olik seemed almost amused. "Oh, it scare me plenty," he said, some of the boom returning to his accented tones. Then his features hardened again. "Everything here scare Olik plenty."

"Really?" Xavier clearly wasn't convinced. "'Cause you seem real calm, man. And you know things, right? You know about her," he said, gesturing at Karen. "You know who I am. But who are you? What are you doing here?"

Olik sighed. "I am just Olik."

"Last name." Xavier was close enough now that he could have reached out and touched the bigger man with his knife.

Olik sighed again. "I am Olik Vardanisdze."

The tip of Xavier's knife faltered. Not much. But visibly. Jim looked at Adolfa. He cocked an eyebrow as if to say, do you understand any of this? She shook her head, a quick back-and-forth that was barely more than a shiver. But enough. She was in the dark, too.

"Vardani...." Xavier's knife dropped a bit more.

"Yes," said Olik. "And I wouldn't do this." He gestured around the car. "There is no percentage in it."

Then both men spun to face Freddy as the wounded man yipped and twisted around. What was left of his mangled hands whipped around like black and red windmill arms.

"What now?" whispered Adolfa. Jim couldn't think of an answer. He just patted her hand.

Freddy yipped again. Spun again. He sounded for all the world like a dog being pinched by merciless children.

A third yelp, and this time Freddy added a short shout: "Stop it!"

Xavier and Olik looked at each other. Olik cocked an eyebrow as if to say, "You see? I'm not touching him." Then both backed away from Freddy as if in unspoken agreement to get away from whatever danger zone had enveloped the unlucky passenger.

Jim almost didn't understand what they were worried about. He couldn't comprehend what would be worse than what he had seen already happening to Freddy.

Surely the worst is over, he thought. Things just *can't* get worse.

But as soon as he thought that he remembered his mother, chiding him for saying something like that when young. "Don't say things can't get any worse," she said. "Don't ever say that. It's like a dare to God."

And she had been right. Look what had happened to *her*, after all.

Freddy spun around like a dog chasing its tail. His trench coat flared. "Stop it," he said. He looked pleadingly at the other passengers. "They're touching me," he said. "Make them stop touching me." His voice, always annoyingly whiny, was now so wheezy it was almost a mockery of human speech. "They're *touching me, make them stop!*"

Jim looked at Adolfa again. He wondered if his eyes looked as terrified as hers did. Probably.

Then Freddy stopped spinning. He screamed and stood up straight, rigid. At first Jim couldn't see any reason for his pain.

Then he did. A trickle at first, barely noticeable. A thin line of red that appeared at the right corner of Freddy's mouth. Blood. Just the tiniest bit, and Jim still couldn't understand why Freddy was screaming – louder, in fact, than he had when his fingers had been pulverized and melted by whatever acid had destroyed them.

Then the quality of Freddy's scream changed. It didn't gurgle or hiss, the tone didn't raise or lower. It was as though the shape of the man's mouth, the sound tunnel through which the scream issued, was somehow altering in shape. Jim looked around, wishing he could keep his eyes off what was happening, knowing he would look back; *had* to look back.

Humans are drawn to horror, he thought. We read it in books, we watch it on movie screens. We slow down during traffic accidents to get a good look. We obsess over the latest celebrity shooting, the latest news of death and destruction. And on the off chance that there is no such macabre occurrence in the offing, we just wait a minute and *someone* will commit *some* atrocity. It's as though humanity can't exist without horror, without fear. Without hopelessness battering at them.

He looked back to the rear of the car. The sound of Freddy's scream was still shifting. The trickle at the corner of his mouth had grown. Blood was streaming all around his lips, in fact. Not like it was coming from inside his mouth, though, but like it was coming from inside the lips themselves, like the capillaries within them were rupturing and the blood somehow pouring through the skin.

A tearing sound pulled through the air of the car, through Jim's ears and mind. Freddy's scream reached a crescendo, a fever-pitch.

Freddy's lips tore off his face.

Jim almost couldn't believe what he was seeing. Surely if someone on the street had told him about this, he would have recommended some heavy medications.

Am I mad? Have I gone insane?

The lips came free, exposing Freddy's scarlet-stained gums and red-running teeth. The man was still rigid, though whether with pain or because he was being held there by some invisible force, Jim couldn't tell.

Jim tried to follow the lips as they flew off Freddy's face, but he couldn't. One second they were attached to the weasely man's face, the next instant they flew into the air in a spray of spit and blood, and then...

... they were gone.

They didn't flip out of sight somewhere in the car. Jim didn't just lose sight of them. Rather it was as though somewhere a few inches away from Freddy's body they had... *shifted* was the best word that he could think of. They had shifted from *here* to *there*. From the place where Freddy screamed to the place where the cause of his screaming had come from.

Xavier and Olik turned and took three quick steps, retreating in a fast but orderly way, like soldiers leaving unexpectedly hostile territory. They drew even with Jim and Adolfa, then turned back to look at Freddy.

The hunger to view horror is universal.

Freddy fell to the floor, his fingerless hands hitting the steel with a horrid, wet *thwop*. He looked up at his fellow passengers, and Jim realized absently that Karen had crept up to join the rest of the passengers. She was still holding her satchel protectively in front of her chest, but she – like Olik and Xavier – had apparently decided that the only safe place to be was with the group. Perhaps the same genetic coding that required human beings to immerse themselves in terror at every turn also required that they do so in the presence of their fellow travelers.

Freddy's lipless mouth opened and closed. His teeth clacked together, and blood drooled down his chin.

Jim thought, insanely, that Freddy would never be able to eat another lollipop. You need lips for lollipops.

"*Hep me,*" said Freddy, the words distorted and odd. "*Shtop them.*"

No one moved. Freddy's teeth clacked.

He screamed again. Again Jim couldn't see why, couldn't see what was occurring now. Olik muttered a soft curse – he was the first to see what was happening. It was like what happened with Freddy's lips. Only this time the blood was appearing at the corners of Freddy's eyes. Weeping blood, like a blasphemous recreation of a holy miracle.

Adolfa whispered, "*Santísima Virgen.*"

Freddy's mouth started pouring blood at the same moment. No trickle this time, but a fountain of crimson. "*Sh-sh-shave m-m-me,*" he managed to stammer. Then there was a triple-tear, three shearing rips. Two small puffs of blood and one large one.

Jim tried to follow what came away. Again he couldn't. Again the objects *shifted*. They went from *here* to *there* and were gone. Gone, but not forgotten. Gone, but not before he saw what they were. Gone, but not before the image of Freddy's tongue exploding whole from his mouth was burnt forever into Jim's mind. Gone, but not until after he saw the other man's eyelids ripped away, leaving forever-unblinking orbs staring in terror and pain.

Freddy's face was a mask of blood. He tried to crawl to them. He couldn't even scream, just made a terrible *ung-ung-ung* sound that was worse than any screaming.

Freddy stared at them all with eyes made far too large by their exposure, with a mouth running blood like a crimson fountain.

"*Ung-ung-ung.*"

Xavier and Olik backed away until they knocked into Karen. Jim felt a strange looseness at his center and knew he was about to lose control of his bladder.

"*Ung-ung-ung.*"

Freddy reached out. And the flesh of his fingerless hand began to peel away, to shear off in long strips like he was being flayed by some unseen knife.

Jim started to scream. Adolfa shrieked as well. Xavier began muttering every curse word Jim had ever heard of and a few he had never known existed. Only Olik and Karen were silent.

The flesh peeled from Freddy's hands. When it got to the hem of his trench coat, the coat itself fell to pieces, revealing a man wearing a Green Lantern shirt and a pair of Bermuda shorts that were far too bright for comfort. Jim's stomach roiled at that for some reason. He was still screaming. So loud that he couldn't hear the noise Freddy – or anyone else – was making.

Freddy's shorts and shirt fell to pieces as well. He was wearing only ratty briefs underneath, stained and dirty-looking. Then those, too, were gone and he was nude.

And still the flesh pulled from his bones. Skin first, leaving glistening red muscle. Then the muscle itself. And not just hands anymore. Arms, feet, legs. Freddy's genitals were ripped off him in a spray of blood –

(*how's he alive how's he alive he's bleeding everywhere so how is he alive let him die someone please just let him die let him die!*)

– and then the only skin on his body was that on his face and head.

Jim couldn't keep screaming. He stopped, and a strange numbness crept over him.

This isn't real. It can't be. Things like this don't happen to people.

Then there was a deep shredding noise. Freddy, still screaming his tongueless scream, jerked. The skin of his body, like everything else, had disappeared, and now the muscles of his calves and forearms tore free of the bones.

Here to *there*, and the muscles and tendons and ligaments were gone. Bare white-yellow bone and cartilage was all that remained.

And still – impossibly – Freddy screamed.

The muscle and flesh of his upper legs and upper arms came next. Freddy fell to the floor, laying in a pool of blood and the soaked remains of his clothing. His head was still tilted up to look at his fellow passengers, his forever-open eyes staring at them pleadingly.

The flesh pulled off his trunk, baring ribs and organs. The organs of his lower trunk spilled out, intestines and kidneys and liver sliding across metal...

... and then no longer *here*, but *there*, and gone.

Freddy was still screaming. Still screaming even when his heart was pulled from his ribcage, still screaming even when his lungs were yanked free.

"How is this?" said Karen. She sounded strangely like a little girl, no longer the high-powered lawyer but instead a young child who has found out that the monsters are not in her closet but instead rule the world.

No one answered her.

There was one final crackling noise. The entirety of Freddy's skeleton seemed to implode, as though caught in an invisible trash compactor. His head, too, started to warp and distort.

But he still screamed. His eyes still stared. Still pleaded for help. For mercy. For anything.

For anything.

But there was no help to be had, no mercy to be given. Jim watched like everyone else as Freddy the Perv's head was compressed to half its normal size. The eyes bulged, the brains started to press out of every orifice.

The head was a quarter-size, then one-eighth. Then gone. Gone, but still Freddy screamed. Somehow he screamed.

And the subway continued on.

5 FARES

Maddie was digging in the backyard yesterday. Well... in the tiny space we call a backyard. I should have been mad – she dug up one of the begonias I just bought.

Before I said anything she explained she was going to plant a tree and we needed a tree because she and Mommy had decided to live in a treehouse someday like the Swiss Family Robinson.

I got Carolyn and we all put on gloves and helped her dig. We'll buy a tree later today. It will die, but that's not important. She'll have her tree for a while.

ONE

The screaming finally stopped. At

least, Jim was fairly certain that it did... but he couldn't be *absolutely* sure. Because he kept hearing it. Kept hearing phantom echoes of the sound in his mind. Kept hearing Freddy shriek "They're touching me" and then dissolve into a pool of blood and cloth and nothing.

He could tell the others felt like that, too. That they wanted someone to reassure them that what they had just witnessed had never really happened; that it was in their imagination, and that they could find comfort in the knowledge that they were merely insane.

But no one could offer that encouragement, Jim knew. Because if one of them was mad, then they *all* were. They were all in this thing together, they were all here experiencing this, and no one could say, "No, don't worry, I didn't see a thing."

After the screaming stopped bouncing off the plastic-and-metal walls of the subway car, no one moved for a long time. Even Xavier, who seemed compelled to express himself at all times – either with profanity or with his knife – was utterly silent. Each person who remained standing sank to the closest seat, as though taking comfort in the hard embrace of the poorly molded plastic.

Surprisingly, Adolfa was the first one to move. She squeezed Jim's arm and then got up, moving around the car. She tried the side doors, but only half-heartedly. Jim understood that: even if they *did* open, what would she do, jump out? The whine of the motor had continued to grow higher and higher. The lights outside were skipping by so fast they looked like lasers, continuous neon blurs that Doppler-shifted from color to color as they passed.

After pulling on the doors Adolfa wandered, apparently without goal or intent, before stopping in front of one of one of the windows. She looked at the various advertisements and public service announcements and bits of graffiti that coated most of the free surfaces on the car before finally settling before one of the maps on the walls that showed the train route. She stared at the bright colors, the circles and squares and numbers and letters as though they might hold some key to what was happening to them.

Olik moved next. He shifted to sit next to Xavier, and started murmuring into the other man's ear. Xavier didn't seem to hear him at first, but after a moment he began to nod. Then they moved to the front of the car and continued to converse in whispered tones, looking back at the others from time to time. Jim worried about that. He also knew there wasn't a damn thing he could do about whatever they were planning: he was just a normal guy, just a person hoping to get back to the two people who mattered most to him. Not a superhero or a Navy SEAL or someone with any hope of taking on two well-armed and clearly dangerous men.

And Karen... Karen stared straight ahead. Her eyes followed the flashing lights that streaked past the windows, but nothing else on her body moved. She seemed to be withdrawing into herself, and Jim thought it very likely she would be completely catatonic before much longer. And though it was tempting – extremely tempting

– to just leave her alone and let her take care of herself, he finally slid across the subway car until he was sitting beside her.

"You okay?" he said.

"Why do you care?" Her voice was still deep, till sexy, but under it he could detect a jagged edge of madness, a cliff's edge that she was dancing far too close to. Or perhaps not dancing, but leaning over. Contemplating a leap that would end some unknown pain by casting her beyond reason's grasp, beyond the clutches of sanity or rational understanding. And he understood that: where there is no sanity, there can be no pain. It is only the sane who can truly suffer.

"That's an honest question," he said with a chuckle. "Aside from the milk of human kindness that runs thick through my veins?" Karen looked at him. Her expression clearly showed where she thought people could put their milk of human kindness, and how long they could leave it there. Jim tried to chuckle again, but it turned into a cough. His throat was dry. He suddenly wondered what was going to happen if people started getting hungry and thirsty.

If we survive long enough to get hungry and thirsty.

"Okay," he said, "how about I care because if you go nuts that's one more thing *I* have to worry about in here?"

She snorted. Then looked at him. It was a frank, appraising look of the sort he was unused to. People in modern society were taught to hide themselves. Honesty is the best policy, except when actually communicating with people. Then be oblique. Be opaque. Lie a bit, because the truth is far too frightening to share in polite company.

That was part of what he loved about Carolyn. She was a no-b.s. kind of gal. And it looked like Karen was cut from that cloth. Again he realized how beautiful she was. Crimson still stained her hands, still dyed the sleeves of her outfit, but she had wiped away most of the blood from her nose where Olik had punched her. And she was gorgeous.

"You're a good man," Karen said abruptly.

Like her stare, the directness of her statement caught Jim somewhat off guard. "What makes you so sure?" he said. It was the only thing that came to mind, but it was also a *good* thing, because he realized that it was the kind of question that would get the woman talking, get her out of the funk she had been in danger of slipping into.

Karen shrugged. Her stained fingers tightened again on her satchel. "Part of my job."

"Lawyer?" he said.

"Acquisitions," she said with a tight smile. "I have to know people." That frank look returned, like a jeweler looking at a gem for possible purchase. "And you're a good man."

He shrugged. "I try."

"I like good people. They're predictable."

Again her statement caught him off-guard. "So are bad people."

She nodded. "I like them, too."

"Just not people in the middle?"

Another nod. "Something like that."

"You going to be all right?"

She looked toward the back of the car. The violet smears and crimson-soaked bits of cloth that were all that was left of Freddy. "I don't think that's an option for any of us."

Jim forced a smile onto his face. "Think positive," he said.

"You one of those New Age nuts who believes happy thoughts can cure cancer?" she said.

"No, but I think positive attitudes keep us sharper than despair."

She nodded at this, as though conceding a point in a debate. "You a shrink or something?" she said.

"What makes you say that?"

"You talk like a shrink." She closed her eyes and inhaled deeply. She looked like she was consciously trying to assert control of herself. "And I told you – I know people."

Jim smiled. "I do come into contact with a lot of... troubled people."

"A shrink." Not a question this time. Karen almost smiled.

The lights went out again. Xavier cursed. Adolfa hurried back toward Jim and sat beside him. He held her hand. Human contact in the face of the unknown. Maybe it wouldn't stop whatever was happening, but then again, maybe it might. Who could tell?

At least it wasn't pitch black this time. The maintenance lights could still be seen outside the cars, streaking past so quickly that each looked like a continuous strip of illumination rather than an isolated patch of brightness in an otherwise dark tunnel.

Then the lights outside *did* dim. Not like they were losing power, or like the windows were growing opaque, but in much the same way that the sun dims when a cloud passes in front of it. Like a shadow was moving around the car.

Jim thought he caught sight of something. He flicked his gaze to the side, but whatever it was, it was too fast for him to spot.

"What is this?" Olik muttered. He sounded worried. So even the imperturbable Georgian had been rattled by the way Freddy had – well, *died* seemed like too tame a term for what had happened to him. Even *murdered* didn't seem to capture the violence, the mayhem.

"Don't know, bro," said Xavier. Jim noted the term of familiarity. He wondered what the two men had been talking about while he was chatting with Karen. He suspected it wasn't anything that would bode well for the other passengers.

There! He turned quickly in the other direction. Almost caught a glimpse of it this time. Was that a hand? A palm pressed against the glass of one of the windows? Jim didn't think that could be possible – after all, what kind of person would be able to hold onto the outside of the rocketing subway car? – but that was the impression left in his mind after his eyes saw only darkness and the continuing sizzle of the outside lights in whatever tunnel to nowhere they had found themselves.

The others were turning this way and that as well, and there were muffled gasps and gulps. Jim suspected they were all seeing – or *not* seeing – the same thing he was. Bits and pieces of nothing. Impressions of hands slapping at the glass. Palms pressed on the outside of windows on a train going far too fast for anyone to be holding on outside it.

"We gonna do this, bro?" said Xavier.

Olik looked at the gangster. Then at the others. Something creaked, a dry but familiar sound, and Jim realized it was the sound of Karen's fingers tightening on her leather satchel. She was scared. Not only of what was now happening outside the subway car, but of what the two men within might be talking about.

Where are the real monsters? Are they outside the car, or in here among us?

Jim couldn't answer that question. He hoped the only thing he had to worry about was whatever was causing this strange nightmare. But looking at Olik and Xavier, he couldn't be sure.

The movement outside continued. Just out of view. Hands, pale in the flashing lights, gone as fast as they had come. And now a flash of hair, long but thin and unkempt. Again, gone before Jim could gather more than an impression of what he was seeing.

Olik nodded at Xavier. The thug reached into his coat, then stopped when a sound shattered the silence of the car. Jim looked toward it. Everyone did. And he knew what he'd see. Before he looked, he knew.

The door at the front of the car, the door that had been locked, the door whose glass had turned dark as the deepest pit.

It was open.

TWO

=====================================

=====================================

Xavier and Olik looked at each other, and it didn't take a psychiatrist to know that they were having some kind of silent pow-wow.

"Check it out?" said Xavier.

"I think so, yes," said Olik. Xavier stepped toward the open door. The Georgian reached out one of his ham-sized hands and grabbed the gangster around the bicep. "Send one of the others first," he said.

Xavier nodded, then turned to the group. "I need a volunteer," he said.

Jim looked away. He thought he had seen something outside. Not just a hand this time, but a face. A pale girl's face, mouth open in a silent scream. He got the impression of a teenager, a girl who had once been beautiful but was now... something else. Something ugly. Terrifying in a way that only lost beauty can be.

Of course, when he looked, the girl – if that was what it had been – was gone.

"You. Thank you for volunteering."

A chill ran up Jim's spine. He was sure that Xavier was a murderous psychopath. Just as sure that the man had chosen him to go first into the next car while Jim had been looking at the window. He looked back.

But Xavier wasn't pointing at Jim. Wasn't even looking at him. He had his strong hand wrapped around Adolfa's wrist. "Get up, Gramma," he said.

"Let me go," said Adolfa. She knocked at Xavier's hand with her small fists. She might as well have been punching a mountain. "Let me go!"

Xavier yanked the old woman to her feet. Pulled her toward the gaping maw of the open door. Olik followed.

Jim looked at Karen. "We should do something," he whispered.

Karen didn't move. "Be my guest," she said.

And again, Jim didn't know what *could* be done. He could rush the two guys, he supposed, but didn't know what that would accomplish. Both of them were dangerous men, both of them were armed and proficient with their weapons.

"Dammit," he muttered.

Karen laughed, a short bark of a laugh that held no humor in it.

"Please," Adolfa was pleading. "*Por favor, mi hijo.*"

"I ain't no one's damn *hijo*," said Xavier. He had his knife out, and he poked her with it. Not hard enough to do permanent damage, but obviously hard enough to convince her to move faster. Adolfa threw a terrified look over her shoulder. She locked eyes with Jim.

Jim felt himself half-rising from his seat. "Guys," he said.

"Sit," said Olik. The huge man didn't even glance back at him.

"We're all better off if we work together," said Jim.

"*Sit,*" growled the Georgian. And now he *was* looking at Jim. And pointing one of his guns at him. The bore of the weapon looked big enough for Jim to fall into.

Jim melted back onto his seat. He felt ashamed. Looking at Adolfa, he wanted to ask her forgiveness. But a large part of him was also glad that it hadn't been him chosen to go first. He had to live. He had to get back to Carolyn and Maddie.

Xavier and Adolfa were at the open door to the next car.

"What you see?" said Olik.

"Nothin'," said Xavier. "Too dark."

"What you mean too dark?" said Olik. "What of lights outside?"

"I mean what I said, bro. It's black in here." He pushed Adolfa with his knife again, and again she yelped. Even in the dim car, Jim could see the back of her outfit stain with blood. Not a huge amount, but it was clear Xavier wouldn't mind stabbing the old woman if he thought the situation demanded it, or if he thought doing so would aid him.

Sociopath.

The word flew into Jim's mind. Someone who didn't have any sense of empathy, who only valued his own purposes and goals. Someone who would do anything to get ahead and who would refuse to see any faults in himself – any problems encountered would be seen as the result of others' shortcomings. Someone with no conscience, no sense of right or wrong beyond what would bring him what he wanted. Jim knew about sociopaths.

And from what he was seeing, Xavier certainly seemed to fit the bill.

Adolfa took a last, quivering look over her shoulder, then stepped into the space between the two cars. She paused on the platform, and Jim felt his heart lurch to a stop with her. He almost expected something to reach down from above and grab her, some tentacled beast from a place beyond Heaven and Hell, a thing that existed only to kill and to feed.

He suddenly felt that he was never going to see the old woman again.

Xavier jabbed Adolfa's back once more. She cried out. Hobbled forward. Bent and almost broken-seeming. To Jim she suddenly looked much older than she had, even though it was dark and he could see her only from behind. As though her will, her sense of self, had been shattered by this moment.

Adolfa stepped into the next car. The darkness that lay beyond the threshold of the open door to the car swallowed her up as completely and utterly as if she had been dipped in an inkwell. One moment she was there, the next she was gone from sight.

Xavier looked back at Olik, whom he had clearly accepted as some sort of *de facto* leader. Olik nodded.

Xavier stretched forth his knife. He prodded at the darkness with the tip.

Nothing happened.

He moved into the darkness, bit by bit. His hand followed the knife. He hissed.

"You okay, Xavier?" said Olik. He sounded genuinely concerned.

"I'm fine, man," the thug said. He sounded angry, pissed that the others had heard him in a moment of verbal weakness. "Don't worry about me, worry about you."

Olik gestured at the darkness beyond the car. "What you feel?"

"I dunno, it's like –"

Then Xavier's words cut off as he was bodily yanked into the darkness. And like Adolfa, he, too, was gone.

THREE

Jim looked at Karen. The lawyer was just staring at the darkness, her face impassive. He didn't know how she could appear so calm. Freddy had literally disintegrated right in front of them, and now two more of their company had been pulled into some kind of black hole in the next car – a car that held God-only-knew what horror within it.

"Xavier?" called Olik. "Xavier, my friend?" The big man was bent over, calling into the darkness of the next car as though he was leaning over a bottomless pit.

Maybe that's what it is. Maybe the whole train is some kind of pit. Or shaft.

But where does it lead?

Jim thought about Freddy's eyes. Staring to the last. But not sightless, not dead as they should have been. Surely they should have been looking at nothing there at the end with all the blood he had lost, to say nothing of the trauma of having his body completely skinned and the meat ripped from his bones. But he *wasn't* dead. He had been alive. Alive, and painfully aware, even when his head was squeezed to a fraction of its correct size. Even when his brains had spurted from his mouth and nose and ears.

Even then, Freddy had been awake, and alert. And in agony.

Dear Lord, what's happening?

Something interrupted Jim's musing. Just as well, since he felt himself spiraling into a depression. And he couldn't afford that. He had too much to live for. He had his girls, and when he saw them again he was going to hold them tight and it wouldn't matter that they'd fought, the important thing was that they would be together again.

It was a hand. Coming from the depths of darkness of the next car, pushing forward as though with great effort, forcing itself through the black wall that separated the car Jim was in from one that had apparently swallowed Adolfa and Xavier.

After a moment, Jim recognized the hand. Mostly because of the wickedly-sharp knife it held. It was Xavier's. The hand pushed through the darkness, followed by the gangbanger's arm up to the middle of his bicep. Then it stopped. The hand started waving frantically, so fast it was almost jerking.

"What's going on?" said Karen.

Jim shrugged. "Looks like he's saying 'come on' or 'hurry up.'"

She looked at him, then back at Olik. The Georgian gestured them forward. "Go."

Jim stepped forward in tandem with Karen. "Why doesn't he call for us if he wants us to come?" he said.

"I don't know. But then," she gritted her teeth in a macabre imitation of a grin, "I haven't understood anything that's happened since the lights went out on this damn train."

Xavier's arm looked dismembered, ending as it did in sudden darkness. Like it had been hacked off mid-bicep and was now being waved around by a ghost with a sick sense of humor. But regardless of what was doing it, the arm now started shaking even quicker: *Come on, move it, get over here, get moving, move faster faster faster FASTER!*

Karen and Jim shared a look.

"I don't think we –" began Jim.

"Shut up," said Olik. The nearly imperturbable man sounded on the edge of losing it for the first time. His deep voice cracked. "Move." He stepped close to Jim, poking him with the gun he still held. "*Move!*"

The gun ground into Jim's ribs. And even though he knew it was only in his mind, Jim felt like the weapon was hot, like it was burning him. He wouldn't be surprised to find a circular scar where the gun touched his body.

It felt horrible. It also felt familiar, as though he were experiencing a premonition of his inevitable end.

He stumbled forward. Toward the darkness. Toward the waving arm.

Jim stepped out of the last car. For a split-second he thought about just hurling himself off the train. Throwing himself into the tunnel and hoping for the best. But of course even that was impossible: the platform between cars was completely enclosed, like an airlock between two different hostile environments. No way to escape. The only options were backward, into the death of the car behind... and forward, embracing the darkness of the car ahead.

As soon as he was within a foot of the black wall that rose like a perfect line of vertical night, the thing that was like a dark force field between this car and the next – between this *world* and the next – Xavier's arm suddenly snapped forward. Jim screamed reflexively as the man's hand clamped down around his wrist, yanking him toward the darkness.

Jim felt his own hand fling back. He didn't think about it. Just grabbed for something, *anything*. Like a man falling off a mountain, grabbing for his fellow-climbers, not worrying that the act of reaching for them might lead to their deaths as well. In the instant of falling the human animal does not think about the other, it thinks about itself. It thinks about stopping its plummeting descent. So Jim reached out. Felt something. Grabbed it.

Xavier's arm was strong. Jim couldn't have resisted him even if he had been ready and waiting. As it was, he just stumbled forward. Touched the darkness.

And felt like the world was ending as he passed through it, and went from one terror into another far worse.

FOUR

"GET UP!"

Someone was screaming, screaming. But it took a moment for Jim to realize who it was, who was doing the screaming, who the person was screaming *at*.

It's me, he realized. He's yelling at *me*.

A moment later he felt a hand practically ripping him to his feet. Xavier. It was Xavier. "Get *up*, man!" shouted the gangbanger. Then he let go of Jim and grabbed at something else. Jim looked behind him and saw Karen on the floor of the subway car. He realized he must have grabbed her when he was pulled through into...

... what?

No time to take in the details right now. Because there was a very seriously pissed off Olik on the floor as well, rolling around like a cross between a rabid bear and a turtle who can't quite get back to its feet. Karen must have pulled him through, Jim realized, just like he did to her.

So we're all together again, he thought. Still one big happy family.

"Get outta the way!" Xavier was screaming. He grabbed Olik unceremoniously by the waist of his pants and hauled him forward. Jim saw that the Georgian's legs were still hanging out into the no-man's-land between cars. But not for long: with one yank, Xavier had Olik tumbling ass over elbows the rest of the way into the car.

Olik grunted as he hit a bank of seats with bruising force. He sprang to his feet almost instantly, both guns in his hands, his face a mask of rage.

"What you think you're doing?" he bellowed, training the guns on Xavier.

Xavier didn't even seem to notice the twin cannons pointed at him. He had his hands on the small lip of the subway door that was protruding from the steel bulkhead. Pulling on it with all his might. "Help me," he said. "Help me, dammit!"

Jim felt his brain spinning like a drunken top. "Where's Adolfa?" he said. His words sounded slurred. His brain fuzzed. He didn't know if that was an effect of passing through the dark wall, or just sensory overload. Either way, he was having trouble processing things.

"I'm here," said a familiar voice.

Jim looked toward the sound. It was the old woman, huddled at the other end of the car. Looking terrified.

Thuds. Movement. Jim looked back at the doorway he had just stumbled through. Saw that Olik was now helping Xavier pull the door shut. And then Karen joined them, as though heedless of the fact that only a moment ago she had been forced through that very door at gunpoint by these men. She knelt below Xavier and dropped her satchel in order to pull on the door as well.

Jim looked up. Shook his head. What's going on? he wondered.

Then he realized that he could see through the door; that whatever power had kept them from seeing into the car, it did not keep them from seeing out. It was like a one-way mirror. Only in this case it wasn't a reflective surface on one side, it was a fathomless plane cut from deepest space.

But from this side... from this side they could see into the car they had just come from.

They could see what was coming *for* them.

FIVE

Zombies. That was the first thought that came into Jim's head when he saw the shuffling mass of people in the car that they had just exited.

The second thought that popped into his head was, Where did they all come from?

Then he realized that question was second to the issue that mattered most: survival.

They weren't zombies. They couldn't be. But they were something bad. Something monstrous and evil and deadly.

They were young. Or *had* been young, before... whatever happened to them. Most of them, he saw, were women. No, not women: girls, young teens. Were they the figures he had seen clambering along the outside of the train before? The ones he had glimpsed out of the corners of his eyes? He didn't know how that could be possible. But then, what of this day so far fell into the realm of possibility?

The girls – at least fifty of them, with a few teen boys mixed among them as well – weren't paying attention to Jim, or to any of the people in this car. They were standing around something in the rear car, the one Jim and the others had just come from. At first Jim couldn't see what the things were fixated on, but then he realized: they were standing where Freddy the Perv had been. Where he managed to both disintegrate and explode.

The girl-things looked emaciated. Used. Dead in soul if not in body. Their skin was scabbed and gray, diseased and lifeless. Their hair hung in lusterless locks, their scalps easily visible in large areas where the hair had thinned or fallen out completely.

Only their eyes held something like life. They shone with a feral need, a hunger. They focused on the circle of gore at the back of the rear subway car. And when the things that had once been young girls had completely circled the blood-spattered area that marked Freddy's demise, they all fell as one and began lapping up the gore.

"Where they come from?" said Olik in a whisper, still trying to pull the door shut.

"Dunno, man," answered Xavier, panting. "I went through and looked back and saw 'em, like, in the back of the car. Just there. Freaked the shit outta me."

"And you not come back for us?" said Olik.

"Tried. Couldn't. It was a like a force field was in the way. All I could get through was my arm."

Olik grunted as though to say, "Interesting," but didn't spend any of his breath on speech. Just bent his back to pulling the door. Jim thought about trying to help, but couldn't see a place to squeeze in between the three people already pulling at the car door. And part of him was too stupefied at what he was watching to move. It was sickening. Fascinating. And on a basic, primal level, somehow familiar.

How can it be familiar? You've never seen this before. Never seen anything *like this before.*

But he couldn't deny it. Like he was looking at a nightmare he had once had, a half-remembered dream made suddenly flesh, Jim felt as though he had seen this before. Or at least something like it.

Beyond the still-open door, Jim saw two of the girls pick up opposite ends of one of the shreds of Freddy's trench coat. They looked like they were maybe fourteen years old. No older than sixteen. Young bodies, barely beginning to change to womanhood. But their skin didn't contain the translucent beauty of youth. It was gray and corrupt, flaking and disease-ridden. It looked like the skin of corpses long-dead and even longer-forgotten. Open sores festered on their cheeks, and Jim thought he could see things crawling in the sores – maggots, or some other carrion-feeding insects.

The two girls gripped the ends of the shred of Freddy's coat and began chewing it. Not chewing *on* it, not like a dog with a rubber toy, but actually eating it. Like a grotesque mockery of the famous spaghetti scene from *Lady and the Tramp*, the two girls started chewing their way towards one another.

They reached the center of the bloody rag/rope. When they came within an inch or two of one another they seemed to recognize each other's existence for the first time. Teeth still clamped around the gory cloth, they snarled. Their eyes bulged, their jaws clenched.

Then they jumped at one another. The girl on the left – a girl who might once have been a beautiful young blonde girl but who was now a gaunt figure with mangy hair and thick clusters of sores around her lips – immediately got the upper hand. She coughed out the bit of Freddy's coat she hadn't consumed, and as soon as she touched the other girl – a skeletal brunette with eyes sunken so deep in their sockets they had almost disappeared – she clamped onto the other girl's face with her teeth and began chewing.

The brunette shrieked, but it was a wet, weak scream. And it terminated as, with a triumphant shout, the blonde literally tore the brunette's face free from her skull.

Jim gasped.

"Animals," whispered Olik. The huge man looked like he had just witnessed the Apocalypse. "What could turn them into animals like this?"

The blonde girl who had won the fight returned to slurping up the scattered patches of blood and cloth that were all that remained of Freddy. Jim expected the other girl to fall. The front of her head was literally nothing but a skull and teeth, red and raw above a ragged blouse that was now stained by blood and bits of skin. But she didn't fall, barely even seemed to notice her wound. The brunette girl just crawled to a different spot in the car. A blood-stained tongue snaked out from between her denuded teeth and jaws, and she joined the rest of her sisters and brothers in licking the floor clean.

Xavier didn't stop trying to pull the dividing door shut, but he coughed suddenly. He sounded like he was trying not to vomit.

The small horde of ghoulish things in the last car didn't seem to notice. They were still licking up Freddy's blood, still eating the last bits of his clothing.

What happens when it's all gone?

Apparently the same thought occurred to Karen. "I think we need to hurry, guys," she grunted.

"Yeah," said Xavier. He was pulling so hard that Jim thought his coat might split right up his back. But the door wasn't closing. Like it didn't want to close. Like it had a mind of its own and was actively resisting them.

And maybe that's not too far off, Jim thought. Maybe this whole *train* has a mind of its own.

Then he realized that would mean that the vehicle was a monster... and they were in its stomach. A long metallic digestive tract that perhaps they had only begun to pass through. And that thought was every bit as disquieting as the sight of the rotting girls and boys eating the remains of what had once been a human being.

Another fight erupted in the back car, this time between two girls and a boy. Like all of the others, the figures looked like they had once been young, perhaps in their early teens. But whatever force had brought them here and wasted their features had also leached any youthful vigor from them. What remained was only rot and hunger, a rabid need to feed cloaked in decomposition and disease.

A lust for blood.

The three were fighting over a bit of cloth. Each held it with a hand, each unwilling to let go. Like the two girls before, the three jumped at each other, teeth clicking as they snapped at one another's faces and throats. This time, though, the fight spilled over into the rest of the company of ghouls.

Soon all were embroiled, screaming, slashing out with fingernails that were cracked and broken into sharp shards. Blood splashed, flesh flayed.

But Jim noted that the blood that spilled from the things in the car was different from the blood on the floor, from Freddy's blood. It was darker. Feculent. Like it had stopped pumping long ago, and had simply lain and rotted in the kids' already-dead veins.

Suddenly there was a click, and the subway door released. "There!" Xavier grunted. The door closed a few inches.

At the same time, Olik said, "Damn." Jim looked and saw that the huge man had cut himself on something when the door released. Red blood streamed down his palm. Tiny tributaries branched off the main flow, racing one another to the edge of his hand.

Olik, Xavier, and Karen kept pulling at the door. It kept resisting.

One of the red trails won the sprint to the lower edge of Olik's meaty palm. Blood gathered there for a moment, curling into a tight crimson ball. Then the ball loosed itself into the air, a single drop that plummeted to the metal of the car floor.

The drop touched the floor soundlessly. There was no tremor, no hint of any change in the air that Jim could sense. But at the instant the blood touched the car, the brawling ghouls in the car beyond the door instantly stilled. They were all wounded by now, some of them so badly that Jim would have thought – under ordinary circumstances – that they absolutely must lay down and wait to die of their wounds. There were limbs lost, bowels that drooped in looping coils behind some of them. But their injuries weren't stopping them; weren't even slowing them down.

And now, as the drop of Olik's blood on the floor was joined by another, and then another, the zombies all turned their heads toward the slowly-closing door. They seemed to notice for the first time that they were not alone.

"Close door!" shouted Olik, and his face grew bright red with the strain.

"I'm trying, man!" screamed Xavier.

Jim watched in horror as the teen-things, faces and bodies raw and bloody and maimed, opened their mouths as one. Their teeth, like their fingernails, were neglected and half-rotten. They had become splintered shadows of themselves, pointed shards that looked wickedly sharp.

They screamed. The scream was like a single voice, a lone entity that spoke through many mouths. A beast that knew nothing of pain or fear or love or empathy. Only hunger. Only feeding.

The ghouls shuffle-ran toward the door.

And Jim knew – absolutely and certainly – that there was no way the door was going to be closed in time.

The things – the things that didn't notice when their faces were torn off, when their arms were ripped from their bodies or when their guts yanked out – were going to get into the car with Jim and his fellow travelers. And the things were clearly very, *very* hungry.

SIX

=================
=================

Jim felt like the blood in his veins had been replaced by quick-drying cement. He couldn't think, couldn't move, couldn't so much as *breathe*. The sight of a horde of snarling, shuffling, snapping things that might once have been high school-age kids moving his way was almost too much for his mind to cope with.

He wondered for an insane moment if he would have had the fight with Carolyn and Maddie if he had known the day was going to turn out this way.

Thought of his girls snapped him out of his stupor. He wanted to see them again. To whisper sorry and I forgive you and I love you. To hold them and never let them go.

He couldn't die here. He couldn't.

Jim sprang forward. He thought he might lend a hand pulling on the door. Might add his strength and perhaps with his help the group could pull door shut and secure it before the horde fell upon them. But that was foolish. Only a moment before he hadn't moved to help because there hadn't been room, and that hadn't changed. Xavier, Olik, and Karen were pulling, screaming and shrieking with the effort. There was no room for Jim.

So what was he going to do?

Karen let go. She started to crawl away. Whimpering. And that was when Jim knew what he *could* do. "No you don't!" he shouted. He shoved her back into place.

"We're not going to make it!" she shouted. She tried to pull away from him.

Jim didn't think about anything but Carolyn and Maddie. Their faces hung before his eyes for an instant, and the next thing he knew, he was reaching into Olik's jacket. The big man grunted but couldn't stop pulling on the door, not even when Jim pulled one of the man's guns free of his shoulder holster and then ground it into the back of Karen's head. There was no time for them to change places; it had to be her. Her or they were all dead.

"Pull, dammit!" he screamed.

Karen shrieked in fear. But she kept pulling. The door closed, inch by inch. And the things beyond the door came toward them, foot by foot.

It was going to be close.

Jim saw the blood on the floor, the spots where Olik's cut had dripped. He thought of the things fighting over the grotesque remains of Freddy. Then he moved again, slamming his hand against the back of the nearest seat. He hit a hard ridge of plastic. The seam slashed through the back of his hand, and he felt a hot rush of pain as blood coursed from the cut.

He took three steps back to Karen, Olik, and Xavier. "Duck!" he shouted to Xavier. Xavier did, and Jim pushed his hand between the gap between door and jamb. He flicked it, and droplets of dark blood flew into the rear car. They disappeared from sight almost immediately, but out of sight was not out of mind in this instance: the ghouls immediately lifted their noses like starved prisoners of war who have just smelled a three-course meal. They fell to their knees, snuffling and licking at every surface they could find.

"Good, good!" shouted Olik, returning to his position and continuing to pull. The door was almost shut.

Then one of the things, a ghoul that looked like it might once have been a redheaded girl of sixteen, suddenly threw itself toward them.

It moved with more speed and alacrity than the others. Whether that was because she had gained strength from the feast of Freddy, or because of "natural" prowess, or some other reason, Jim couldn't say. But she was ten feet away one moment, and in the next, Olik was screaming.

The scream was surprising, both in its suddenness and because it turned the man's voice from a deep bass to a high soprano. It might have been comical in other circumstances. Not here, though. Not now.

The redhead grabbed Olik's hand, the one that was still on the outside of the subway door, and began chewing it. Like Freddy's coat, Jim could tell there was no intent to simply bite it for effect: the thing was resolutely attempting to eat Olik's flesh, to swallow it whole.

Olik's scream rose, rose, rose. He fumbled with his other hand, reaching in his coat. Not finding what he wanted.

Xavier stood, pulled out his knife. He reached around the door. Slammed the knife through the redheaded girl's eye. The eye seemed to pop, gray jelly and too-dark blood splatting down her cheek. Xavier grunted and pushed, and all six inches of the blade disappeared into the girl's head. Deep into her brain.

It didn't seem to bother her in the slightest. She grunted. Bared her teeth, which were clamped around Olik's three smallest fingers and part of his wrist.

And she kept chewing.

Olik drew breath. Screamed again. Another scream joined his. It was Karen, shrieking but not letting go of the door, still pulling it shut.

The rest of the things in the rear car started to stand. Apparently they had licked Jim's blood clean. They moved toward Olik, who was spurting the precious fluid now, his blood coating the floor between the cars.

Olik was still fumbling in his coat, and finally managed to get at what he had been trying for. He pulled out his second gun and unloaded a flurry of shots at the redheaded ghoul. She jerked and shuddered as each slug entered her. Even in his distress Olik aimed precisely, placing the rounds in the ghoul's head and face. And Jim realized that the bullets must have been some kind of soft- or hollow-points, because each one seemed to take off half a pound of flesh as it passed through the ghoul's head. By the time Olik emptied his magazine it was nothing but jaws and hanging shards of skull and flesh.

But the thing kept chewing. Gnawing. *Eating.*

Xavier looked at the rest of the things heading at them and returned to pulling at the door. He looked at Jim. "Shoot him," he said.

"What?" Jim said. Shook Olik? He felt numb. Overloaded again.

"Shoot him, man!" screamed the gangster. "Shoot him and buy us some time."

"No!" shouted Olik.

Karen pulled at the door. Screaming wordlessly. Her eyes seemed blank, like she had checked out mentally.

"Don't do it," shouted Olik, and put another shot through the shredded nub of bone and teeth that were all that remained of the ghoul outside the car door. He almost sobbed. "It won't let go."

"Shoot him!" shouted Xavier.

For a second, Jim couldn't figure out why Xavier was telling him to shoot Olik. He had almost forgotten that he was holding Olik's other gun. Then he looked down. At the gun. At Olik. At the horde. They were almost there.

"Don't," whispered Olik. "I fix this." He dropped his gun. Empty. He held out his hand to Jim. "I fix this."

"Shoot him!" screamed Xavier.

Jim thought of Carolyn. Maddie. He only had a moment.

SEVEN

Jim handed over the gun.

It was part decision, and part preordination, a strange sense of fate that gripped him in that instant, as though no other choice were possible or permitted. He felt like a puppet with strings kept tight, a thing of flesh but no will.

So Jim handed Olik the gun, and the big man pushed it out the ever-shrinking crack of the doorway, and pointed it. Jim saw what he was doing through the thick glass window, and didn't have time to realize what the Georgian was doing before the man pointed the gun and inhaled sharply.

Olik didn't point his gun at the ghoul that was still eating its way up his hand. And it made sense that he wouldn't: gunshots hadn't done much thus far. No, instead Olik pointed his gun at the point where the thing was doing the chewing. At the juncture between the monster's flesh and his own.

Olik took a breath, and Jim had an instant to wonder at the other man's guts, at his insane bravery. He wondered if he would be able to do what was coming if he had been in the big man's place. If his survival instinct would be so strong.

Olik pulled the trigger. There was a roar, and another of the man's high-pitched screams, and then he fell into the subway car, free at last from the teeth of the ghoul.

Olik's left hand was a mass of blood and flesh that looked like it had been run through a meat grinder. Between the effects of his own bullet and the young ghoul's teeth, there was little left of it: pretty much just a thumb, one finger. The rest was just stringy bits of sinew and bone poking out of a ragged purse of skin.

Jim took a step, thinking he might help with the man's injury. Olik shook his head, teeth gritted. He pointed at the door with his good hand. "Close it!" he shouted.

Jim nodded, and took the spot Olik had vacated.

As Olik had done, Jim had to grab onto the door with both hands, one on each side. His left hand tingled as it passed onto the side of the door where the ghouls fought and screeched and lapped at Olik's blood. He could feel the air of them, the fetid fumes coming off them in almost visible waves.

But none of the zombie things seemed to notice him. Or rather, they noticed but didn't care. Not while there was blood at the ready. And there was plenty. Olik's blood seemed to be all over the inside of the door and the flooring between the cars. The ghouls crawled over and around themselves like human-shaped grubs, lapping at every drop of blood. Their sore-crusted skin was within easy reach of Jim, their snapping teeth within mere inches of his exposed hand.

"Come on," said Xavier.

The door continued to move. But slowly. Jim didn't know if it would finish closing before the things finished licking up the last dregs of Olik's blood. And when that happened... then what? Would they stand silently? Would they remain calm and simply wait until blood flowed again?

Somehow he doubted it.

As if in answer to his unspoken question, some of the child-fiends – the ones that were farthest from him, the ones who had no access to Olik's blood, or who had already lapped up what blood they could reach – started to hiss and spit and bite at one another. The horde started to roil, to become a teeming mass of violence.

The door was almost closed.

The nearest ghouls reached for him. With fingers, with *teeth*. Jim could almost feel their jaws clamping on his hand.

"Pull, dammit!" He didn't know who screamed, if it was him or Xavier or Karen. It didn't matter.

A finger touched his. A caress that was soft, so soft it was almost obscene, like the touch of a lover come to call, the first tentative kiss of a long-absent sweetheart. "Let me in," the touch said. "Let me in and you will know... *delight*."

Jim screamed in revulsion and fear and – worst of all – in a kind of long-buried yearning. As though part of him hoped for death at the soft touch of the creatures on the other side of the door.

He pulled. The door inched toward the metal jamb.

And then suddenly the door was closed enough that he was able to switch his grip so that both hands were on the inside of the door. He didn't think he'd ever been more grateful of anything in his life.

Dead gray fingers started to reach around the door. Then hands, grasping, clutching.

Xavier and Karen had also switched their holds, pushing with their full combined strength on the door, forcing it shut. Now Xavier let go of the door with one hand long enough to hack at the intruding hands and fingers with his knife. Some of the hands withdrew. Some of the fingers he cut off, and they remained on the inside of the car, crawling like sightless grubs, mindless worms that still carried an impossible hunger within them.

The door shut. Xavier pulled off his belt one-handed and used it to lash the door to the nearest seat supports.

Jim didn't let go. He knew he'd have to at some point, but he didn't trust that this was over. It *couldn't* be over.

He looked through the window.

The things were there. Standing just beyond the glass. No longer fighting, no longer attacking one another. They simply stood with their pus-ridden bodies, their scarred skin and their dead eyes and lank hair.

And they stared.

Waiting.

Jim looked back at Olik. Adolfa had moved up at some point and was now helping the big man bind up what was left of his hand. It looked like she was using a ripped piece of her skirt.

Xavier let go of the door. Gingerly at first, clearly waiting to see if his belt would hold the door shut, then stepping away with what looked almost like defiance.

"I think it's gonna hold 'em," he said. Then he yelped as he stepped on one of the still-squirming fingers he had cut off with his knife. He kicked it away, disgust rippling across his face.

Jim heard something. A sound he hadn't heard much of before this night, but one that was so distinctive that he would never forget it.

A gun being cocked.

He turned and saw Olik, holding his gun. Pointing it at Xavier.

"You told him to kill me," said Olik. His bass tones were back. His face had always been white, but rage and loss of blood had turned it to a shade that was almost blinding, even in the near-darkness of the subway car.

Jim's stomach crawled, because whether the door held or not, he realized anew that the monsters in the car behind were not the only ones he had to worry about. There were other monsters in the car right here with him.

He wondered if he would ever live through this. If he would ever see his girls again.

And suddenly he was possessed by a feeling so strong it was more like a premonition, a prophecy, a sure knowledge. A conviction that the fight he had had with Carolyn and Maddie would be the last he ever saw of them.

EIGHT

Jim had watched both Olik and Xavier move. Under normal circumstances, he thought Olik was the more dangerous person. That suspicion was born out by the fact that Xavier had seemed – for whatever reason – to defer to the big Georgian, and Jim suspected that Xavier wasn't the type to defer to anyone he didn't fear.

But this was hardly a normal circumstance. Olik was down, badly wounded and almost certainly in shock. Jim didn't know if Xavier analyzed those variables. Probably not. The gangster probably saw the weapon and simply reacted. But regardless of whether the gangbanger's move was calculated or instinctive, it was effective.

Xavier threw himself to the side. Olik managed a pair of quick shots, but both went wide. Another sign of the bigger man's incapacitation: the fact that he missed, a far cry from the perfect groupings of shots he had been able to squeeze off earlier.

Jim noticed this only peripherally. Primarily he was involved in his own survival. He dove for what cover there was, hunching down and throwing his hands over his head in the classic "Please-God-save-me-I'm-screwed" position. He saw Karen doing the same, then lost sight of most of what was happening around them as he buried his face in his hands. Another shot cracked out, and a bullet zinged off metal somewhere nearby. Then there was only the sound of scuffles, the noise of close-quarters survival: heavy breathing, thuds, grunts.

Jim looked up after a moment, the need to know what was happening overcoming his animal desire to hide. He saw Xavier on top of Olik, the gangster wrestling with both hands to keep the bigger man from pointing his gun at him. Then Xavier twisted and brought his elbow sharply around, cracking it into Olik's cheek.

The Georgian barely seemed to notice the hit, but it did distract him long enough for Xavier to hammer his knee down on Olik's mangled hand. *That* Olik noticed. He screamed, and lost control of the gun. Xavier tore it away from him. Hit the bigger man with it. Again, Olik seemed barely to notice.

Xavier hit him again. And again.

The third time, Olik's body seemed to accept the fact that it was being pistol-whipped into submission. The big man finally started to lose consciousness, his eyes rolling back in his head. He kept struggling, but the fight oozed almost visibly out of him.

Jim wondered if he should help. Wondered *who* he should help.

But then it was too late. Xavier hit Olik one more time and the Georgian's eyes closed.

Xavier stood, fist clenched around Olik's gun. He was breathing like an ox in heat, his cheeks slick with perspiration. "What the *hell's wrong with you?*" he screamed, and kicked Olik's unmoving form viciously in the side. Olik moaned but didn't regain consciousness.

Xavier looked around, and Jim shrank from the man's gaze. The gangbanger looked like he had taken a bad drug trip, like the fight with the ghouls and then with Olik had been the straw that broke the back of his sanity. He pointed the gun at each of the remaining passengers in a hand that trembled enough for Jim to fear the man might accidentally discharge the weapon, but not so much that he thought Xavier might miss if he decided to shoot someone purposefully.

"What's wrong with *all* of you?" he spat. "You," he said, pointing at Adolfa. "You, what've you done to help, Gramma-*cita*? Other than run away and be a pain in my ass?" He swiveled to point the gun at Jim. "And you, you white-ass, sniveling *pussy*. Only thing you been good for is to close that door there. Other than that, you done nothing. *Nothing!*"

Then the gun turned on Karen, who was still hunched in a corner. A glint that Jim didn't like came into Xavier's eye. "And you. Stand up." Karen didn't move. "Stand up!"

Karen did, but seemed like she barely had the energy or balance for it. She was whispering something under her breath. Jim couldn't make it out.

"I seen how you been looking at me," said Xavier. "All high and mighty and so much better than me. Well you ain't better than me!" He licked his lips and added, "Not better than me." Those words were quieter, but somehow they seemed more dangerous to Jim, like the hush that seemed to come into the air before a vicious lightning strike.

Xavier's eyes flicked over Jim's shoulder. Jim couldn't help himself. He looked. He knew he shouldn't, knew he should keep his eyes firmly glued on the gun and the deranged man holding it. But he glanced behind him.

The ghouls were there. Watching. Standing clustered around the lashed-shut door to the subway car. Their eyes seemed to glow in the hazy dim, illuminated by the searing glow of the lights that passed by outside the car, the red and white and yellow and green lights that would have seemed almost Christmasy in other circumstances, but which now simply cast everything in macabre and sickly tones.

The girls and the few boys were not moving. Just watching. Watching.

Waiting.

Jim was thrown back to the moment he looked down on his mother. Seeing her body for the first time after... after it happened. The blood. Wanting to touch her, wondering if she was dead. Knowing she was. The sense of expectation, the sense of dread. He wondered suddenly if his eyes had looked like those of the things that now watched the strange drama in the subway car.

Jim looked back at Xavier. The gangster's eyes had lowered a bit. No longer looking at the ghouls outside the car, but at the door. Or no, at....

"My belt," said Xavier. A sly grin spread across his lips. The grin made Jim feel like vomiting. It reminded him for some reason of Freddy. But a version of Freddy

119

grown large and strong and dangerous. A predator who had graduated beyond ravaging helpless children.

Xavier's eyes moved to Karen. "Bring me my belt," he said.

"What?" She looked at the door. As if to remind her what the belt held back, the door rattled slightly as the ghouls pressed against the lashed door. "Are you insane?"

Xavier stepped closer. He cocked the gun. "Bring me my belt, bitch!" Karen didn't move. Xavier's grin grew wider, more cunning. Jim's flesh felt like it was going to crawl right off his bones as Xavier's free hand dropped to his jeans. He hitched at them. "Then *you* come here."

Karen looked shocked. Confused. Jim knew what was coming, and wondered if she did. Wondered if she knew but refused to admit it. "What?" she said again, her eyes wide and uncomprehending.

"Come help me with my pants, bitch," said Xavier. "They're falling down."

Karen looked at Jim. He saw now that she understood; saw a request for aid in her eyes. And he wanted to help her. He was a good guy. He prided himself in that, it was something he had hung to his whole life.

But he also saw Maddie. He saw Carolyn.

Was it better to die a hero, or to return to his girls?

He didn't move.

"Get over here, now!"

Karen stepped forward with a sob. Her feet moved strangely, hitching forward as though they were had been stuck in tar, like she had to jerk each one free before taking a step. Xavier watched her approach with clear relish, his grin no longer physically capable of widening, but somehow managing to grow more intense. The lights outside began streaking by more rapidly, the laser-like glints illuminating his sweaty face and the rapid flare of his nostrils.

"You don't have to –" began Adolfa.

"Shut up," rasped Xavier. He didn't look at her. His eyes remained glued to Karen, gleaming like those of a jackal. Jim wondered if this had been the man's intent from the beginning, from the first moment he had laid eyes on the woman. Jim knew about rapists, about sex crimes and the types of people who committed them. And he suspected that Xavier was the type called a sadistic rapist, a man who, once inflamed, might not stop until he killed or at least maimed his victims.

Karen was almost within reach of Xavier. Jim wondered again if he should do something. Try something. And again he saw his girls. Saw their faces in his mind.

He wasn't being weak. He was being smart. He was trying to survive for them.

He almost believed it. Almost believed the lie he was telling himself.

Xavier's hand shot forward with the speed of a striking viper. He grabbed Karen by the arm and pulled her closer, placing the muzzle of Olik's gun against her throat.

"Get on your knees." Karen shook her head. She sobbed. "I won't say it again."

Slowly, slowly, Karen lowered herself. Xavier switched the gun so it was pointed at her eye. She dropped her head, and now it was pointed at the top of her skull. Which was no consolation, Jim thought, since any angle at this range was an assured kill shot.

Jim caught Adolfa's eye. She looked terrified. And like him, she looked totally incapable of anything more than watching.

"Undo my pants," said Xavier. He laughed. "Should be easy. Belt's already off for you."

"Please," whispered Karen. Her voice was so low, so breathy, that Jim could barely hear it. It was the dream of a prayer, the last gasp of hope.

"I saved your life, bitch. With my belt, I saved your uptight, rich ass that's so much better than mine. So now I figure you owe me."

"Please," she said again. Even more quietly.

Xavier's smile disappeared. Rage flared across his face with the white-hot intensity of a sunspot. His free hand snapped out in a vicious punch that hammered Karen's already-bloody nose into a pulp, that knocked her senseless and possibly killed her where she knelt.

Or at least, that's what Jim figured *should* have happened.

NINE

========================

========================

Xavier was fast. So fast his fist was a dark blur in the blackness of the subway car. So fast that the lights outside illuminated him only partially, like an old movie with frames missing. One moment he was standing before Karen, holding the gun to her head; and the next instant his fist was swinging toward her at something approaching the speed of sound.

But as fast as Xavier was, Karen was faster. As brutal and violent and devastating as his attack was, hers was more so.

Moving so quickly Jim could barely make out what she was doing, Karen leaned back and to the side at the last second, allowing Xavier's fist to pass by her face so close that it ruffled her hair. At the same time, her hands snapped up and slapped the gun. Jim didn't see what she did, but there was a sharp crack and Xavier screamed.

"You broke my fingers!" shouted Xavier. The gun fell from his hand, and Karen scooped it out of the air.

"That's not all I'm going to do to you," she said. The quaver was gone from her voice, the terror had absented itself from her eyes. In its place was... nothing. No fear, not even anger. Just a terrible void that Jim found even more terrifying than Xavier's homicidal rage.

Who *is* this woman? he thought. Who are *all* these people?

Xavier pulled his knife out with his good hand, and slashed at Karen. She was still on her knees, and Jim would have guessed that would put her at a severe disadvantage. But she didn't seem to mind her position. She brought up the gun and used it to blunt Xavier's knife attack, then rolled back effortlessly, a backwards somersault that put a few feet between them and ended with Karen back on her feet again.

The instant she was up, Karen fired two quick rounds. It didn't look to Jim like she even had time to aim. But Xavier screamed and lurched forward as both his feet more or less exploded. His knife fell from his hand and he lurched toward Karen, arms pinwheeling as he tried to find his balance atop feet that suddenly ended about two inches before where his toes had once been.

The knife slid across the metal floor of the subway car and stopped at Jim's feet. He swept it up and shoved it into his waistband, not thinking about using it as much as about keeping it away from Xavier.

Xavier was still stumbling toward Karen. She waited until the last second, then stepped calmly out of his way. She kicked Xavier in the back as he went by. He screamed, a guttural shriek that seemed like he had been wounded even worse by the kick than he had by the gunshots. A moment later, Jim saw why: the kick had buried the spike-heel of Karen's expensive boot a good two inches in the muscle of Xavier's lower back. The heel had broken off there and now jutted out of his back like a tent stake, just one more insult to his injuries.

Xavier went careening by Jim, still unable to stop his headlong fall down the aisle to the back of the car. Jim scuttled away from him, half jumping, half crabwalking.

Jim didn't know what was going on, didn't know how Karen had managed to avoid death or worse. But he did know that wounded animals were often more dangerous than they had been when healthy and whole, so he gave Xavier as wide a berth as possible.

He didn't go all the way to Karen, though. Because she still had that dead look in her eyes, that terrible void where a soul should be. And that scared him even worse than the possibility of being hurt by the wounded and angry gangbanger.

Xavier finally came to a stop, sliding on the stubs of his now half-complete feet and slamming into the back window of the subway car.

The ghouls, still there, still watching, had their hands against the other side of the glass, fingers wide as though reaching for him.

Xavier bounced off the window face-first. He hit it so hard it cracked. Blood splashed across the glass and he bounced off the door then fell hard beside it. He moaned.

The ghouls on the other side of the door started licking the glass, trying to get at Xavier's blood that now dripped in thin lines only a few millimeters beyond their reach.

"Get up," said Karen.

Xavier's only answer was another moan.

Karen pulled the trigger on the gun. The suppressor whiffed and as if by magic a ding appeared in the floor only a few centimeters from Xavier's crotch.

"Shit, woman!" he half-shouted, half-cried. "You gonna blow my nuts off."

"Eventually," she said. Her eyes looked like black holes in the darkness of the subway car, like they had fallen away from her skull and left only pits behind. "Get up."

"What...?" someone mumbled. Jim realized Olik had regained consciousness at some point. He was sitting halfway up, looking around with a dazed expression, though Jim couldn't tell if that was because he was concussed or just confused at the turn of events that had just taken place.

Karen glanced at Olik, then focused her dead gaze back at Xavier. "Get up," she repeated.

Jim felt like he was watching a tennis match performed at light speed. His eyes whipped back and forth, trying to look at both Karen and Xavier at once.

Xavier groaned. Then screamed as Karen fired another shot and another inch of his right foot disappeared. "Get up," she said. "Or I'll kill you one tiny piece at a time."

Xavier was crying now. Jim thought it was a strange sight, the tears running down the tough man's cheeks, streaming over the four tattooed tears under his eye and then mingling with snot and spit that dripped to the floor as he tried to push himself up.

He wondered how many men and women had faced Xavier like this. How many had wept, how many had begged for mercy. Had pleaded with him for their own sakes, and the sakes of their families.

And how many had received the mercy they prayed for.

Not many.

Then Jim frowned. It was still dark in the car. Still black in the shadows. But he thought he saw something move. Something... *there!*

At first he couldn't figure out what they were. They looked like some kind of strange grubs or sickeningly thick worms, their bodies bloated and distended by a bellyful of blood. Then his stomach lurched as he realized. Realized what they were.

He saw it in his mind, the memory of Xavier's hand flashing out. Just a moment ago –

(*had it been a moment, or forever? it seemed like forever, how long have we been here?*)

– cutting at the ghouls that tried to get through the door, slashing at their hands, slicing at their fingers, hacking them off.

Hacking them off.

Jim looked at the grotesque crawling things he thought he had seen in the minute flashes of illumination provided by the lights outside the subway. There! There they were again! And no, they weren't worms, weren't grubs.

They were fingers.

The dismembered digits moved along the floor like sickly slugs, searching for sustenance in the evernight of the subway. And they had found it. Had found their way to the blood that trailed from Xavier's ruined feet.

"Please," whimpered the gangbanger, unaware of the things wriggling toward his prostrate form.

"I'll count to five," said Karen.

"You'll kill me no matter what," said Xavier.

"Yes," she said. "But there's dead, and then there's *slow* dead." She took a step toward him. "One."

Jim opened his mouth to say something, but he didn't have a chance. He thought the ghouls' fingers would take a few seconds to work their way forward, but they were fast. So fast it shocked him. It was impossible – not that any of this *was* possible – but the things suddenly lurched forward. They seemed to clamp onto the hashed edges of Xavier's mangled feet. Jim had an instant in which he glimpsed something, an impression of something strange and toothy, and then Xavier started screaming.

"Shut up!" shouted Karen. Her eyes remained empty.

Xavier didn't shut up. He kept screaming. Jim saw the things, the finger-teeth-worm things, disappear into the raw meat-wounds of the rapist's feet. Xavier's scream took on a new, more strident, jagged tone.

"Get it outta me!" he shrieked. "Get it outta me!"

Karen frowned. "Stop it!"

"Get it outta me!"

Jim moved away from Xavier. He didn't want to be next to Karen, but he wanted to be near whatever was happening to the rapist even less.

"Get it outta me!"

Karen fired the gun again. Another bullet wound appeared, this one tearing off a portion of Xavier's right hand. He didn't even seem to notice.

But Jim noticed the things that seemed to swim out of pools of darkness under the seats, fingers and thumbs that oozed out of shadow and then lurched to the unfinished stump of Xavier's hand.

"What... what are those?" said a dazed voice. Olik.

"What...?" said Karen, clearly about to echo the sentiment.

Just as had the ones Jim saw earlier, the bits of flesh launched themselves at Xavier's bloody tissue. Again there was the momentary impression of teeth, of grinding, burrowing maws. Then the ghouls' invasive fingers slid inside Xavier's hand, burrowing their way into his wounds.

Xavier's screams reached a range and decibel level so high that Jim expected the windows of the subway to shatter. Expected to feel blood spurting from his eyes, his brains sliding through his ears.

Then, under the scream, he heard another sound. He couldn't figure out where it was coming from at first, then realized it was coming from beyond the closed door to the back car. The ghouls.

He looked through the windows. The ghouls were panting. Their dead eyes closed, their mouths open. Their wounds, still wet and dark and oozing, seemed to pulse in the lights that flashed by outside the subway train.

They moaned. Not like they were in pain, but rather like they had found themselves captured by deepest pleasure. As with their screams before, the moan seemed to be singular, an individual sound somehow issuing simultaneously from dozens of throats.

The sound was low, keening. Orgasmic.

"Get it outta me! I don't want it in me!" Xavier's panicked cries grew more strident, and as they did the ghouls' panting grew more pronounced, more heated and deeper. As though they found sexual release through whatever was happening to the man.

Then Xavier threw his head back and screamed louder than before. His back arched.

Jim felt something and almost jumped out of his skin before he realized it was Adolfa. She had again crept forward. Once more taking comfort in the group.

Jim looked behind them. The front door to the car was closed, the window dark. He suspected – knew, somehow – that they couldn't get out there. They were stuck here with whatever was happening to Xavier.

Xavier's screams changed. They started rattling, wheezing. Jim looked back at the man and gaped. He blinked rapidly, unsure what he was seeing. Then sure what he was seeing, but unable to believe it.

"My God," said Olik.

"No," said Karen. "I don't think so."

Adolfa crossed herself.

Xavier's mutilated feet began kicking a speedy tattoo against the floor of the subway car, a *rat-ta-tat-tat* tapping that bounced through the frame of the entire car, through the seats and support poles and through Jim's own bones.

"Don't let it in me," gasped Xavier. But Jim could see that it was already too late for that.

Xavier was on his back now. His stomach grew bloated, distended like that of one of those kids you saw on late-night infomercials about third-world countries, the ones that offered to let you adopt someone for only a buck a day. The skin of the man's belly must have been pressing painfully against the inside of his coat, for he unzipped it with his good hand, gasping as he did so.

Underneath the coat, Xavier was wearing only a T-shirt emblazoned with the logo of some energy drink. It, too, was stretched tight against the huge mound of the man's belly. But at least it was cotton, so it couldn't hurt as much as the constricting coat must have.

"Help," panted Xavier. No one moved. Well, not true. Olik moved: he got slowly to his feet. But neither Jim nor any of the others approached Xavier. They just watched. Jim didn't know about the others, but he couldn't have looked away if he had been offered a million dollars and a way off the train.

Xavier's stomach continued swelling. The size of a basketball, then a beach ball. So big it seemed like it was going to have to burst, blowing Xavier to pieces right in front of them.

Karen took a step back. So did Olik. A moment later Adolfa joined them. Jim followed. Still watching. Still captivated, unable to turn away.

Xavier didn't burst. His shirt tore, ripping right down the middle and exposing a stomach branded with tattoos that had probably once been threatening works of art meant to mark him as a gang member of some renown but which were now distended so far they were distorted beyond recognition. The skin of his stomach continued stretching, stretching. Blood started to seep from it, as though it were tearing at a microscopic level.

"Please," whispered Xavier. Then he started screaming again.

And his stomach, the huge, bloated, cancerous thing, started *moving*. Not autonomously, not like it wanted to pull away and become a separate entity, but more like...

... "What *is* that?" said Karen...

... something was *inside* it.

Xavier put both hands – one whole, one half-ruined by Karen's well-placed bullet – on his stomach. He was still screaming, but the screaming had lost volume, as though his strength were waning. Or being siphoned off by something.

His belly bulged as though something were pushing against it from the inside. Then the bulge split, becoming two bulges. Then three. Jim had a momentary impression of a tail. Or tentacles.

Xavier's screams grew louder again.

The thing inside him was still growing. It was half as big as Xavier himself, an impossibly huge mass attached to him by skin that had stretched farther than was possible. Blood was running down his dark flesh, discoloring the tattoos that marked him, staining the floor around him.

"Help me," he whimpered. "Get it out of me." Then another scream wracked his body.

The bulges pushed around his stomach. Then they moved, converging on a point just below Xavier's ribs. Whatever was inside Xavier seemed to writhe, then burrow *under* his ribs. Jim wondered how that was possible, how the man's ribcage could contain something that size.

The answer came an instant later: crackling snaps ripped through the car as Xavier's ribcage burst outward, inflating his chest to twice, then three times, its normal circumference. But his skin still held. It bled, thick red coursing over and around it from every pore, but it *held*. Like the skin of a balloon, stretched to its limit but not ready to burst.

Xavier's screams turned to coughs. The writhing thing inside him moved up his chest cavity. Jim thought he could see tentacular extremities reaching into the man's neck, which started to swell.

"Help," said Xavier. His voice was a whisper, but his eyes shrieked.

The ghouls in the last car were still moaning, still gasping and shuddering like they were experiencing the most erotic experience of their un-lives.

Xavier stopped speaking, stopped shouting, stopped whimpering. The thing pushed into his throat. Like his stomach, like his chest, Xavier's throat seemed to inflate beyond its capacity. Jim could hear tiny snaps – what must be the vertebrae in the rapist's neck popping like ten-cent firecrackers. He looked at Xavier's feet, expecting to see them loose and limp, the nerves severed at last. But they still tapped that death-dance against the floor.

And yet, though his feet and legs moved, they were at the same time somehow... diminished. So was Xavier's stomach. The thing within him had moved out of his belly, and the skin there hung loosely, as though in passing the creature inside had robbed Xavier of most of his mass, most of his flesh. Indeed, now that Jim watched, Xavier's skin seemed to shrivel and wither. It was like he was mummifying, a thousand years of weathering and aging occurring in a moment.

Jim's eyes went back to Xavier's face. The man's face was still whole. His eyes still screaming and in pain.

The thing was in the rapist's throat. The throat had stretched so far it was wider around than Xavier's head, Jim guessed it had a circumference of at least twenty-four inches. Maybe more. Xavier's head looked like a grotesque pimple at the end of his neck.

More cracking. This time Jim couldn't pinpoint it for a moment. Then he saw that Xavier's mouth was open. Open as though he wanted to scream, but no sound coming out. Open wide. Too wide. He saw the gangbanger's mouth stretch beyond what it should, the corners of his lips growing white as the jaws underneath dislocated. Then the skin tore, Xavier's mouth widening by several inches on each side. Twin pops sounded, like low-caliber gunshots in the dark subway car.

Jim had been riveted by what was happening. So had everyone else, he guessed. Those two pops, though, shocked him into movement. He stepped back. Again.

Xavier's hand – desiccated and dried as though he had been sucked clean by a spider – reached out to Jim. His eyes pleaded with him. "Don't leave me," they said.

But his mouth continued splitting open. Wider. Wider.

And then something *reached out* from inside the man's mouth.

TEN

Jim fell back with a scream of disgust and fear. Everyone did. Everyone but Karen.

Jim saw her face as she darted past. She no longer wore that dead expression, that visage that bore no pity or remorse. She had a visible emotion now: fear.

So why was she moving *toward* Xavier?

At first Jim thought she might be going to end his suffering. The man's mouth was split open so widely that the ends had disappeared around the back of his head. Jim was reminded of a game he had played as a kid: Mr. Mouth, a game where two half-spheres joined at the back by a single hinge formed an impossibly wide mouth that rotated around in a circle as kids tried to flip tokens into it.

Xavier's turned into Mr. Mouth.

Why doesn't she just shoot him?

His thoughts were going everywhere. He was in danger of losing it.

Focus, Jim. Keep cool.

You'll end up like Mom. Just like her.

Keep it together.

Karen darted to the back of the car. Not to Xavier after all. She grabbed her leather satchel, which she had dropped there a few minutes and a million years ago when they had first entered this car. Then she hurried back to the rest of the group.

"What's in there?" asked Olik with a look at Karen's satchel. It was a perfectly legitimate question but one that struck Jim as unimportant considering what was going on a few feet away.

Karen didn't answer.

The ghouls in the final car exhaled climactically. Xavier coughed. Retched. Things pushed out of his mouth. Jim expected to see the ghouls' fingers, the things that had forced themselves into the other man. He figured they would have sucked him dry somehow, would have grown in size and strength and would emerge even hungrier for human flesh.

But he was wrong.

It wasn't disembodied fingers that squeezed out of Xavier's ever-widening, ever-tearing mouth. It was entire *hands*. Tiny, dark, coated with mucus and blood. They pulled themselves out of the gangster's raggedly stretched mouth. Followed by thin arms. Shoulders.

A head.

Black hair, plastered tightly against the skull beneath.

And under the hair....

Jim felt his stomach draw into a frozen knot, felt his testicles pull tight against him. He would have thrown up, but his body knew somehow that to do so would be to use time he did not have. To do so would be to stay and die.

"What is this?" said Olik, wonder and disgust mixing in his voice.

"*Blasfemia,*" whispered Adolfa.

Jim shuffled back. He bumped into something soft. Adolfa. Or maybe Karen. He didn't care. He just wanted to get away.

The tiny arms reached for them. Small eyes opened, and as they did the light at last went out of Xavier's eyes. His withered body relaxed, went limp. But Jim didn't think the man's suffering was over.

The tiny hands....

Olik was whispering. One word over and over, something in his language. A word that could only be a denial, a whispered refusal to believe.

The hands reached... reached for them....

Jim looked behind them. Hoping that the door at the other end of the car would be open, hoping that they could get to the next car.

It wasn't open. But there *was* something there. Standing on the other side of the still-closed door at the front of the car.

The driver. The conductor of the train. The skull Jim had seen driving the subway when all this hellish nightmare had begun.

But not a skull, he saw now. Just a terribly thin man. Old and drawn, like he had been living far too long underground and had suffered terribly for lack of sunlight and open air. His skin was so white it fairly illuminated the space between the cars. The transit cap on his head seemed large and unwieldy on his head.

He locked eyes with Jim. Smiled and raised a finger to his cap. An oddly old-fashioned movement that was beyond insane given the circumstances.

The driver's smile widened. Lights flashed outside the train. The ghouls in the last car moaned at the same moment, and when the light and sound collided, it seemed as though Jim could see the skull again, the skull he thought he had first seen driving the train.

Then the old man stepped back. Stepped back. And, still smiling, disappeared into the darkness of the next car.

The door to the next car slid silently open.

Jim hesitated. Perhaps they would be better off here. Things had just been going from bad to worse, after all.

Then he looked back at Xavier's destroyed form. At the... *thing*... that was still crawling out of his mouth. The dark arms. The nude body.

The tattoos that covered it. Gang signs. Four of the tattoos, on the thing's grotesque, misshapen face, looked like tiny tears.

The thing looked up at them. Looked up at Jim. "Help," it whispered. And the voice was small and weak and pitiful... and chillingly familiar. Xavier's voice.

The rest of the tiny body, the replica that had been born of itself, slid out of its father/self's mouth. Completely nude, it lay in a pool of blood and tears on the cold floor of the subway car. It tried to push up on small arms emblazoned with gang symbols.

Beyond the glass, in the back car, the ghouls moaned.

The small thing screamed. It fell to its back.

Its stomach started to bulge. "Get it outta me!" it screamed. *"Get it outta me!"* The stomach started to move. Its ribcage started to crackle.

The cycle was beginning again.

At the same moment the belt on the back door fell away and the back door opened. The ghouls shuffled in. Moaning with the pleasure of the damned, rubbing their wounds and injuries as though doing so brought them to greater heights of ecstasy. They writhed over and among themselves like an orgy of the dead. They surrounded the tiny thing that had come out of Xavier, that *was* Xavier; that had killed Xavier and borne Xavier and would do so again.

The Xavier-thing shrieked. Its mouth started crackling open. Tiny fingers – even tinier this time – appeared at the corners.

When will it end? Will he get smaller and smaller until he puffs out of existence? Or will this go on forever?

Jim felt hands at his arms. Pulling him. Adolfa? Karen? Olik? He didn't know. He couldn't tell. He didn't want to – couldn't – look away from the thing that had killed Xavier, the thing that had taken his place and become him.

The hands pulled him back.

They pulled him through the door to the enclosed platform between cars. Then to the next car in the subway.

He watched Xavier's eyes. Watched them scream. And knew. Knew, somehow, that for Xavier this was not going to end.

Then the ghouls encircled the smaller body that had come from Xavier and become Xavier and now had another Xavier within him and coming from him. The ghouls moaned in that strange single voice, they writhed over him, they became a creeping, wriggling mass of dead-alive flesh. They sighed and seemed to melt into one another. It was impossible to tell where one body ended and another began. It was an endless round of death and pain, a never ending circle of doom.

Xavier screamed.

Hands – Adolfa's, Jim thought – reached out and pulled the door closed. It slid shut and he heard it latch. Darkness fell in the car beyond it.

But the sounds could still be heard. The sounds of a man dying and being reborn into pain, over and over and on and on forever.

And the subway continued on.

4 FARES

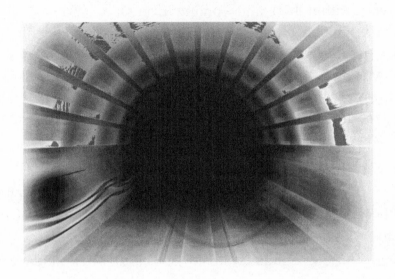

Carolyn was asleep on the couch with Maddie curled up in her arms tonight. Carolyn ate too much banana bread and had to sleep it off, I think.

Neither one was moving, which is rare, especially for Maddie. The girl has more energy than a speed freak.

But tonight they were just there. One asleep, one watching cartoons. I could watch them. It was a perfect moment. My girls.

ONE

This subway car was a bit different than the last two had been.

It took a few minutes for Jim to realize what the difference was. He was still reeling from what he had just seen, from the strange unreality that he had somehow been trapped within. So at first he didn't notice the fact that the seats were no longer hard gray plastic, the poles no longer burnished aluminum. Instead, the chairs were covered by a thin upholstery, a soft cloth that was the same color as the seats in the back two cars had been but seemed much older. And the poles themselves were missing, replaced by simple leather straps that hung every few feet along the length of the car.

Like most New York subway users, Jim knew what a "straphanger" was – it was a name for a commuter, taken from the old days when all the subways had been outfitted with straps just like the ones that hung in this car. But as the more modern cars had been phased into use, the straps had seemed to grow more and more exotic. Like an endangered species, one that now hid in plain sight so that even on the rare occasion when you were traveling in a car that had the old straps, you barely noticed them – and even when they were there, any New Yorker worth his or her salt almost never used them.

So why did it seem like this car had them so prominently? So prevalently? And what was with the upholstery?

Jim took a step and noticed that the floor seemed to be wrong, too. Gone was the dark gray metal of the car they had just exited. This floor was a different shade. Hard to tell in the streaking light that shattered the darkness in laser glints, but it seemed to be dark red, perhaps even the deep maroon of newly-spilt blood.

All in all, it led to a strange sense of age, as though this car had been lifted out of a bygone era and pushed its way into the middle of a more modern train. Only the ads, plastered over each of the windows, seemed to be as modern as the cars they had just come from. But that just added to the strange sense of disconnect, the anachronistic quality of seeing a banner hawking the newest Broadway show on this too-old car making Jim feel almost dizzy.

A strange blanket seemed to lay itself over Jim's thoughts. He could hear screaming. He thought it must be Xavier, or the thing that had somehow both killed Xavier and at the same time *become* Xavier. Then he realized that wasn't it. No, the screams he heard weren't coming from beyond the closed door at the back of the car. They were coming from his own mind. The screams of a murdered mother, the screams of death come to one far too young.

Jim stumbled. His legs felt like the strength had run out of them. Hands gripped him. Guided him to one of the nearby seats. It turned out that the upholstery wasn't much softer than the plastic seats had been. Perhaps worn thin from too many years of use, perhaps never that soft to begin with. Either way, the seats pinched at his legs as though angry to be used this way.

"You okay?" Eyes swam in the darkness before him. It was Adolfa, he realized, almost invisible in her dark clothing. Her grandmotherly face full of concern and a kind of saintly woe that seemed utterly out of place in this train of otherworldly horrors.

"I don't know," Jim mumbled. The only honest answer. He looked around, almost ridiculously proud of himself for managing to complete the movement without vomiting on himself.

Karen was moving up and down the car. There was something odd about her gait, and Jim thought at first that she must have been injured in the flight from one car to the next. Then he realized that wasn't it. It was her boots. One of them was taller than the other.

She left one heel in Xavier's back. Before he....

The thought trailed off into a vague sense of malaise, as though his mind could not approach what had just happened in a direct fashion. Only obliquely, in quick glances. To look at some things too long would be to embrace madness.

But Xavier... he became himself. A smaller himself that became a smaller himself that was becoming....

Jim heard the screams in his mind; the shrieks of the would-be rapist: "Get it outta me!" And then the sickening shredding of his face parting to allow his smaller doppelganger to crawl forth.

Karen stopped her restless motion. Jim focused on her, focused on her and in so doing tried to focus his thoughts *away* from memory. He looked at her form – still beautiful even in the star-streaked un-night of the subway tunnel – looked at the leather satchel that she still carried. He wondered what was in it.

Karen reached out and pushed against one of the windows that lined the length of the car. Her lips pursed with effort, but the window didn't give. She reached a bit higher and pulled on something. Jim couldn't make out what it was at first, then saw it was a cord of some kind. It ran the entirety of the car. An emergency stop cord, he realized. The kind that hadn't been in use for decades.

Where are *we?*

Karen took a few more lurching steps, then frowned and kicked out suddenly. Her remaining heel snapped off against the side of a seat with a crack that made Jim jump. And as much as the sound surprised him he was amazed at the offhand precision of the kick. Even if he hadn't just seen her take Xavier apart, he would have known just from that movement that she was not a woman he'd want to cross in a dark alley... or even a bright alley, for that matter.

Just beyond Karen, Olik was sprawled on another one of the seats, clutching his mangled hand to his chest, a cigarette between his teeth. As Jim watched, Olik pulled out a gold lighter and ignited the cigarette, then inhaled deeply and blew a cloud of smoke into the air. The smoke looked almost white in the darkness, a swamp mist that could lead the gullible or otherwise unsophisticated to believe in aliens.

Maybe that's what's happening. We've been abducted and this is all some kind of weird experiment. We're rats in a maze, being poked and prodded to see what makes us tick, and tock, and – in the end – stop either ticking or tocking.

That made a certain kind of sense. At the very least it allowed Jim to explain some of the bizarre things that had happened. But whether it was the truth or not the explanation didn't get him any closer to freedom, any closer to Carolyn or Maddie.

"What are you thinking of, *mi hijo*?" said Adolfa.

"My girls," said Jim. The train was still bouncing lightly in that way that is particular to trains, passing over the tiny seams between pieces of track, *click-clack click-clack click-clack*. But he suddenly doubted that the track was real. This had to be in his mind. There was no track, there was no train. It was just lunacy, a long dark trip through insanity that ended only in more of the same, a Mobius strip cut from a single infinite length of madness.

Adolfa's eyes looked worried. Like she thought he might fly off the handle and start trying to kill people at any moment.

Maybe he would. If that could end this, maybe he would.

"Tell me."

"What?"

"About your girls. Tell me about them."

Jim knew what she was doing. Psych 101 stuff: deflect attention from things too difficult to bear, get the subject to look at things that provide feelings of comfort, stability, safety. Something to live for.

But knowing what was being done didn't keep it from being effective. Sometimes placebos worked even when you knew they were just sugar cubes.

He pulled his journal out of his pocket, then took the picture of Carolyn and Maddie from its pages. His fingers shook, minute tremors that he suspected would never dissipate, as though terror had been genetically introduced into his DNA.

"That's Carolyn," he said, pointing. "And Maddie. My girls."

"They're beautiful," said Adolfa. Her wrinkled face crinkled still further in a smile. "Especially your daughter. She has your eyes."

Jim chuckled. "She's not my daughter."

Adolfa looked surprised. "But you said –"

Jim shook his head. "The father left when Carolyn was still pregnant with Maddie. I just came into their lives last year. But Maddie...." His thumb moved across the photo, touching the little girl's smile. So different from the last look he'd seen on her face.

Will I ever have a chance to make those things right? To get back to them and make sure they know I forgive them, and that we're all still fine?

"She's like your own," said Adolfa. It wasn't a question. Jim nodded. "Sometimes we get to choose our family," she said. "I have three sons. Two of them...." She made a dismissive motion, like she was throwing out minute bits of garbage. "But the third is *de oro*. Pure gold. Carrying on in the family business, hard worker. And he married a gorgeous girl, *pura bella*. Kim Hill was her

148

maiden name. And Kim has a friend who also came into the business, a boy named Scott Robbins. I know, I know," she said, and smiled as she waved again, overcoming objections that Jim hadn't voiced or even thought of. "Neither of them are *latinos,* but it doesn't matter. They are good people. Hard-working. Trustworthy. Loyal. Loyal above all. To the family."

Adolfa reached out a thin finger and touched the picture in Jim's hand. "It matters not who provided the building materials, it matters only who made something of them, *sí?*"

Jim nodded. "You could be a helluva shrink, you know?" he said.

Adolfa cackled and clapped her hands together. "I'm an *abuela,* a grandmother. Sometimes this is the same thing as being a shrink."

Jim smiled back at her. He didn't feel good – the only thing that would make him feel *good* right now would be a guaranteed way off this subway train – but he felt better. And that was a start.

"So touching," said a gravelly voice.

Jim and Adolfa looked over. Olik stood before them, his face white and damp with perspiration. One hand hung to a leather strap, his body swaying with the subway's movement –

(*click-clack click-clack click-clack on tracks that probably weren't even there not really not in the really real reality and not whatever fake reality held sway here in the dark*)

– and marble-sized beads of sweat rolling down his forehead and cheeks. His other hand, the one that he himself had basically shot off, was tucked partially into his coat. Jim could see the blood-soaked dressing that Adolfa had tied on the shredded meat of the man's hand, and a rough circle of darkness was staining Olik's coat where his bad hand was tucked.

Of his gun there was no sign, but Jim had no doubt that the other man still had it. And that he could draw and use it quickly and without remorse.

Olik must have recognized the fear that clenched Jim's guts, that pulled and pushed his bowels at the same time. The huge man shook his head. "Don't worry. No need to be," he grinned, a smile that Jim supposed was meant to reassure but somehow only managed to put him more on edge, "*uncivilized* about this, yes?"

Olik turned around. He caught Karen's eye. "You. Come join us, yes?"

Karen looked at him. Her eyes didn't have quite the same dead appearance they had when she was efficiently destroying Xavier, but Jim noted they still looked veiled, almost sleepy. Like she was experiencing everything through some kind of filter.

After what seemed like an eternity, Karen spun and shoved at one more window. It rattled in its frame but didn't give, so she turned and walked slowly toward the group. Her boots, *sans* heels, gave her a peculiar gait. It reminded Jim of the way the zombies – or ghouls or whatever they were – had walked. Like they were no longer completely in control of themselves.

Not that any of us is in control of much anymore.

Finally Karen stood before them. She held her leather satchel in one hand, but angled her body so it was half-obscured behind her. Jim wondered if she thought she was hiding it. Then realized that was impossible: unless she had suddenly turned into an imbecile, the woman had to know they were all aware of her package. So why...? Then he realized: she wasn't hiding it, just keeping it as distant as possible from the rest of the group.

He wondered what was inside the bag. What would be so important that it would be worth going back toward Xavier, toward the ghouls, to grab it up before running like hell with the rest of the group?

Jim glanced at Adolfa, then at Olik, and could see instantly that the same thoughts were going through both their minds as well. Karen must have noticed, too, for she fell back into what looked like a half-crouch. Jim didn't know if she intended to run or to attack. Either way, Olik raised his hand once more. "No, lady, no. No fighting. Let's work together." He smiled his unsettling smile again.

"Like we did before?" said Karen. "When you and your boyfriend tried to use us as guinea pigs?" Her eyes lost their dullness for a moment. They sparked. Rage. Then the spark disappeared and that same muffled expression draped itself over her visage again.

"Look," said Olik. "We didn't know what we were going to see."

"We still don't," said Adolfa. "So you going to push us first into the next dangerous place?"

Olik looked almost embarrassed. "I probably would," he said at last. "But...." He lifted out his mangled hand. "Hard to push anything with one hand, yes?"

"Maybe I should just push *you*," said Karen.

Olik's attempt at good-natured appearance disappeared instantly. "Try," he said.

"Wait," said Jim. He stood. Loathe as he was to get between people who had the clear will and apparent skill to kill each other – and everyone else in the car – a dozen times over, he also didn't want to take a chance at being caught in their crossfire. "Let's ease up. Take a breath." He looked at Olik. "What did you want to propose?"

Olik seemed to find that question amusing. "I should call you Nathaniel, yes?"

Jim frowned. "I don't...."

"You are like the man in Bible. Nathaniel of old, who Jesus said, 'Behold an Israelite indeed, in whom is no guile.'" Olik grinned. "You have no guile, little man. Like Nathaniel. You just ask your question, straight and forward."

Jim's head was spinning again. A subway going who-knew-where, with a rapidly diminishing number of strangers... and now one of them turned out to be some sort of macho thug who was a closet biblical scholar?

"What do you want?" he finally said.

Olik looked at the group. "I want to live," he answered. He pointed at Adolfa. "Like you, yes?" She nodded. "And you?" he added, pointing now at Jim. Jim felt his own head bob up and down, feeling almost as though someone else was controlling his actions. "And you?" Olik asked Karen. She didn't answer. Just stared at him. He nodded as though she had responded clearly in the affirmative. "Of course. So we need to work together. Talk. Survive."

"Why do you want to work together now?" asked Adolfa.

Olik smiled that predatory grin of his again. "When I was boy, I worked part of every year as shepherd. Deep in woods, with my brothers." He wiped a hand across his forehead, looking at the perspiration on his palm for a moment before flinging it away. It disappeared into the darkness. "All day long they teased me. Pushed me, punched me. I stayed away from them. But at night... at night I slept between them. And why?" Olik looked around. No one spoke. He wiped his forehead again, his eyes far away for a moment as he relived old memories. "Because at night the wolves came. They howl in the night, and I was afraid. So I sleep between my brothers. Not because they would protect me, but so when the wolves come, they will eat my brothers and I will be able to escape." His eyes refocused. His grin now looked like that of one of the wolves he spoke of. "I don't think any of you will care for me, yes? But I will stay with you, because perhaps you protect me from the wolves."

"Or maybe you'll be the one who gets eaten first," said Karen, her eyes still shrouded by a mist of non-emotion.

Olik's grin didn't falter one iota. If anything it grew wider. "Is what you call a win-win, yes?"

Karen smiled back. But Jim noted that the smile didn't reach her eyes.

Olik turned back to the others. "So we band together, yes?" He put his hand forward. "We fight together. Survive."

Jim stared at the outstretched hand. It was palm down, fingers rigidly forward. He didn't know what to do with it. But a moment later Karen put her hand on top of Olik's.

Good golly, he thinks we're in a football practice.

It was absurd.

But then, was it any more incredible than the events that had already transpired?

Adolfa put her hand on top of Karen's.

A moment later, Jim added his own hand to the group. And when he did he was surprised to find that he didn't feel silly at all. Rather, he felt like he was making a choice that would have fateful consequences. He was choosing his team.

And like it or not, it was the team he was going to play on until this deadly serious game was over.

TWO

═══════════════

═══════════════

"First is first," said Olik. He pulled his beefy hand away and sat down. Slumped almost, his body going loose at the last second as he let himself fall into one of the seats. "Who are you?"

Jim looked at Adolfa. She was looking back at him with a quizzical expression, and he sensed that she expected him to take the lead in the conversation. He swiveled back to Olik. "What do you mean?" he said.

Karen sat down. Rigid. A tightly-coiled spring that might burst into movement at any moment. Jim suspected he didn't want to be around if that happened. "He wants to know details about you," she said.

"Is right," said Olik with a nod.

"Like, our favorite colors?" asked Jim. "Our turn-ons and turn-offs?" He could hear the acidity in his voice, and didn't care. When Olik had pulled his hand away the sense of foolishness had returned. They had no chance. They were children playing in a minefield, and the only question was which one of them would be blown to hell first.

Jim sat down as well and wondered if he wouldn't be better off just staying in a seat until the train stopped or some new monstrosity came for him. Resistance was an exercise in pride sometimes. And sometimes it was worse:

an exercise in stupidity. Sometimes it was better to let fate come, to let death take you.

No. Think of the girls.

"Not turn-offs," said Olik. He laughed loud and long. The laughter was harder than the situation merited, but his mirth seemed genuine. "I mean what you are good at, what skills you have. Things that may keep us alive," said Olik. He didn't seem to take offense at Jim's tone, and Jim had to remind himself that he was talking to a very dangerous man. "For example: I am businessman. Who is very good shot." He patted his coat where Jim presumed his remaining gun was holstered. "I also am good fighter, but with one hand, not so much." Olik looked at Jim. "I hear you talking about being shrink. Is doctor, yes?"

Jim nodded. "A shrink is a psychiatrist. A doctor of the mind."

"But with medical training of the body?"

"Some."

Olik nodded approval. "Good. Helpful. What happened to the little man, and to Xavier... you ever see things like that before?"

Jim shook his head. "I've never even heard of anything close to that."

"And of people who followed us into car?" said Olik. "They were dead?"

Jim paused. "I... don't know." Then he shook his head. "No, they couldn't have been. They had to be alive."

"But they kept coming when they were shot," said Adolfa. Her eyes were wide, fear settling into the shadows on her face. Jim worried she might shut down if she followed that line of reasoning too far.

He shrugged. "Maybe they were on something. Some drug. Like some super-powerful methamphetamine or some other drug I've never heard of. But dead?" Another shake of the head. "That I can't accept." He noticed Olik looking at him with narrowed eyes. "What?" he said.

"Super-powerful methamphetamine?" said Olik, repeating Jim's words, rolling them around for a moment as though sampling their taste. He paused, looking like he was going to say something further, then shook his head and switched his gaze to Adolfa. "And you?"

Adolfa actually grinned, that same wide-open smile that she had flashed on Jim before all this had started. She suddenly looked as though she hadn't a care in the world; as though she was having a conversation with friends on her veranda, and not a strategy session in a bullet train to nowhere. "I'm just an *abuelita*, she said." The pride in her voice was clear.

"Yes, a grandmother," said Olik. "I heard this, too. But even a grandmother must do more." He leaned toward her. To Jim's astonishment the huge man actually looked friendly now, concerned and interested. No hint of threat about him. "What did you do, *abuelita*?"

Adolfa looked around as though uncomfortable being the center of attention. "I... I helped my husband run our family business."

"Which was?" Olik still spoke softly, gently coaxing the information out of her.

"Just a little store," she said. "Little things to the neighborhood children."

Olik nodded somberly, as though she had just told him she was researching cures for cancer. "Where is your husband now?"

Adolfa laughed, a rasping titter that sawed through the darkness of the subway car. "Oh, he died years ago." Tears glittered in her eyes. She wiped them away and sat up straight, a proud woman pushing on with what tools she had. "I took over. I grew the business without him."

Olik nodded. Jim saw him, saw what he was doing. Saw him assuming the role of the father of this strange mixed family. Saw him forging a bond between Adolfa and him. Cheap, basic psychology, but the man was doing it well.

Whatever he is, he's more than a "businessman."

Olik reached out a hand and placed it on Adolfa's shoulder. He squeezed it. "What you do for the store?" he asked.

"Bookkeeping, mostly," she said, dabbing at her eyes with the ends of a sleeve. "Some hiring and firing. Inventory."

Another squeeze by Olik, and Jim saw gratitude bloom in Adolfa's eyes.

He's got her, thought Jim, and couldn't help admire the man's deft touch. She'll die for him now.

"We will find a way for you to help us, *abuelita*," said Olik. "And we will protect you until that time comes."

He turned to Karen. And as he did, Jim noted something. A flash in Adolfa's eyes. It was fast: so fast he couldn't be sure it really happened. Maybe he imagined it, maybe it was just the flare of one of the streaking lights outside.

But he didn't think so. At least in that instant he thought it was something real. In that instant he thought he saw *amusement*. Like *Adolfa* had been the one playing *Olik*.

Then the look was gone and she dabbed at her eyes, just looking grateful for the attention and the promise of protection.

Olik lifted his chin when he looked at Karen. Again, Jim noted the posture change. To Jim he had presented an overbearing attitude, a menace. A subtle threat if he didn't get his way. To Adolfa the man had seemed the patriarch and protector. Now to Karen he was holding himself forth as a fellow-soldier. As an equal – and equally dangerous – peer.

"And you?" Olik said. Admiration crept into his voice. "I've never seen someone move the way you did against our good friend Xavier."

Karen didn't answer for a long time. Then in a near monotone: "I take karate."

Olik snorted. "So you are just lawyer?"

Karen looked at him evenly. "I'm in acquisitions."

"And you take karate, what, after work and on weekends?"

"A girl needs her exercise."

Olik looked like he was trying to decide how much to challenge her on that. He sighed and leaned back. "So we have the brain doctor, the *abuelita*, the ass-kicking lawyer, and me."

"What kind of business *do* you run?" said Jim.

Olik's wolf-grin returned. "Internet commodities."

"Like gold and silver trading?"

"Something like that."

"But not that."

Olik shook his head. "No."

"Then what, exactly?" Jim looked around. "Since we're all in this *together*, like you said."

For a moment he wondered if he had gone too far, if he had pushed Olik's charade of familiarity beyond what the man was prepared to accept. Olik suddenly seemed to swell in his seat, as though he had miraculously pulled substance from the air itself to add to his mass.

This is it. I'm dead. Good-bye, girls.

Then the fight dissipated as fast as it came. The big man relaxed. He leaned back in his seat and kicked out a foot, his posture suddenly that of a man with nothing more to worry about than when to get the next beer out of the fridge.

"My commodities are a bit more… perishable… than gold and silver," he said.

"What does that mean?" Jim said.

Olik chuckled. Amused by Jim's inability to divine his meaning. "You are doctor. Smart man. You tell me."

Jim thought. Internet commodities, the man had said. Like gold and silver, but "more perishable." He had no idea.

Olik chuckled again, a deep rumble that turned into a painful cough. He curled around his mangled hand, still jammed into his coat. Jim wondered how long it would be before the guy needed a hospital.

"Cotton?" said Jim. It was the wrong answer, he knew that. No way was an internet cotton mogul wandering around the subway with a pair of silencer-equipped guns tucked into his jacket, ready to make mince-meat of anyone who got in his way. No, whatever Olik was into was something considerably uglier. Illegal. "Drugs?"

Olik was still coughing a bit, but he shook his head. He was smiling. The smile was starting to piss Jim off. Maybe he wasn't some super-criminal like this guy, but he wasn't a *moron*.

"Sex."

The word seemed to come out of nowhere. It slithered like a serpent out of the darkness, a single syllable that said so much with so little. Jim knew Karen had said it, but only because *he* hadn't, and it didn't seem like the kind of thing Adolfa would say to a bunch of strangers.

Olik looked at the woman with an admiring nod. "You are one bright kick-ass lawyer."

"You sell sex?" said Jim. "On the internet? Like call girls? An escort service?" His voice must have sounded his confusion to Olik. Another of those irritating seismic chuckles bounced out of the big man's chest.

"No, not escort service." Olik leaned toward Jim. In the darkness the big man's fevered eyes seemed to glint. Jim was reminded of the saying that the eyes are the windows to the soul. He wondered if he was glimpsing a very bright avenue in a particularly hot suburb of Hell. Probably. "I trade in *people*. Women. Girls. Boys. You have money to pay, I will ship you the goods. Willing and compliant, with all necessary," he coughed delicately, "pharmacological means to maintain compliance." His grin was beyond wolf-like now. It was rapacious. The smile of someone who profits off suffering, off broken families and loss of innocence... and who sleeps like a baby each night.

Jim felt sick to his stomach. "You call that being a businessman?"

"I call it being very rich businessman," said Olik. "Sex trade powers internet. No people looking at porn, no people like me. No people like me, no more of your precious emails and Googles."

Jim shook his head. "That's not how it works."

"Is exactly how it works." Olik looked relaxed. An expert in his domain. "Average person looking at internet is also looking at porn. Who supplies porn? People like me. And then when they are tired of porn, where do they turn? Also, people like me. Because supply always leads to more demand. I am merely filling a need."

Jim glanced at Adolfa. She looked disgusted, but he sensed she wasn't going to say anything. She was too fragile, too vulnerable. And she had pinned her hopes for the future on the strongest person in the car. At least for now.

He looked at Karen. "Doesn't this bother you?"

Karen looked at him like he was something she would hire someone to scrape off the back of her toilet. She didn't say anything.

Jim looked back at Olik. The big man was smirking. "You see? No one *likes* me. But most people..." and he motioned at Karen and Adolfa, "... they will recognize me as necessary evil, yes?"

"No," said Jim. But he said it without conviction. Like he only half-believed himself. Like maybe Olik was right. Maybe there was necessary evil in the world.

No. That was ridiculous. Jim had always tried to be a good guy. Maybe he wasn't perfect – who was? – but he didn't accept the idea of *necessary evil*.

Olik put a hand on Jim's knee. "You will come around," he said. "Everyone does eventually, yes?"

Jim didn't say anything. There was nothing he could say.

Olik stood. "Okay then: let us look for way out of this place. Before more monsters come for us, yes?"

Adolfa nodded and sprung – all-too-eagerly – to her feet. She didn't want the monsters to get her, that was clear. She wanted to get back to her grandchildren.

Jim stood, too. But slowly. And couldn't help thinking that by signing on to Olik's team he might actually be joining *with* the monsters.

THREE

═══════════

═══════════

Olik didn't do anything magical: he just gave each of them a portion of the car to look at. But at the same time, it was an important change and it gave Jim – and, he sensed, the others – a sense of purpose and hope that had been lacking since the lights had gone out.

He wondered how long they had been on the train. Time had seemed to stretch out strangely. He couldn't be sure if it had been minutes or hours. Surely not more than that – he didn't have to go to the bathroom, so that was a pretty fair indicator that the time period was still short.

But good Lord, it felt like it had been forever.

He moved down his quarter of the car. He pulled at the upholstered seats, wondering if any of them might lift up to reveal a hidden compartment or anything else that might prove useful. They were all securely attached to their bases. The only thing he got when he did that was a handful of dust, as though the car hadn't been cleaned or used for months or years. That fit in with the overall feel of the car, which still looked like it had somehow come through some kind of time tunnel from the 1950s.

Jim thought about that. He wasn't a science fiction nerd. He had never been to a Star Trek convention, had never dressed up like a Storm Trooper or tried to impress a friend with a realistic lightsaber purchased via some geek website on the internet. But he knew *some* things. He knew about worm holes and parallel universes and string theory. Things you couldn't help but know in today's entertainment-saturated world.

Could they have fallen through a worm hole? Could they be in some alternate dimension? Some version of the world where the subway tunnel – and the train itself – just went on forever in a continuous loop?

He rejected the thought as soon as it came. For one thing, it didn't feel right. More important, he had no idea how they would get out of such a situation if that was the case. So he was going to abandon it as a dead end and consider other possibilities.

But what else was there? Alien abduction? Unlikely. Mass hysteria? Unheard of on this kind of level.

Drugs?

That merited some thought. Jim seemed to remember reading of some government experiments with hallucinogens that –

"How am I going to collect for any of this?"

Jim jerked around. He was almost at the center of the car, the spot where the side doors created a gap in the seats that lined the walls. Karen was on the opposite side of the gap, also looking for anything helpful in her part of the car. She looked frustrated, her tan face whiter than usual, her eyes seeming almost to glow in the lights that streaked by outside.

"What did you say?"

Karen didn't stop moving. She patted down seats, pulled on windows. All one-handed. The other hand was still gripping her satchel. That damn satchel, which was starting to annoy Jim beyond reason. He thought that, given half a chance, he would just conk the woman over the head and take it from her.

"I didn't say anything."

"You did. You said –"

Now Karen stopped moving. She stood and stared at Jim. "No. I didn't. And they lied!"

Her eyes bored into his, and he fell back a pace.

She's losing it.

If they didn't get out of this place quickly, he thought it likely that they wouldn't have to wait for some external horror to come for them. They'd fall apart and rip each other to pieces.

Karen clicked the combination lock at the top of her satchel. It popped open. And as much as Jim had wanted to see what was in there only a few seconds ago, he now wanted just as badly to keep the bag shut. The way she held it, he felt like the opening of the bag was a barely veiled threat. He was in danger.

"Look at this!"

Jim swung around. Grateful for anything that might offer a chance to shift Karen's attention away from him. He saw Adolfa near the back of the car. Looking up at something.

"What is it, *abuelita*?" Olik hurried to her, still playing the part of the father figure, or the protective older son watching out for his beloved relative. He put a hand around her shoulder. "You find something, yes?"

Jim cast a last glance at Karen, then moved away as well. "What, Adolfa?"

Adolfa gestured to them all to hurry. Jim heard Karen's distinctive heel-less tread behind him. As soon as he reached Adolfa, she pointed at the small bit of wall above the windows, the space usually reserved for ads and for the subway maps. "Look here," she said.

Jim looked. It was barely visible, but he saw pretty much what he expected. "It's just a route map," he said. Though upon further inspection he saw that the map was one he didn't recognize. The colors of the routes were unfamiliar, and instead of the usual letters and numbers, strange symbols decorated the map. Nor did it end, really. It seemed to get fuzzy at the edges of the pane, like it was disintegrating, falling out of existence without actually ending. But whenever Jim tried to look closer at it, his eyes sort of slid away from it. Like there might be something there, but his brain was unwilling to let him look at it, loathe to let him comprehend it.

Adolfa shook her head. Hope animated her face. "Look closer."

Jim, Olik, and Karen leaned toward the map. Jim still didn't see anything. But Olik did. The big man chuffed like a surprised dog. "What are we missing?" asked Jim.

Olik's big finger reached up and tapped a spot on the map. "Ha!" he bellowed.

When the big man pulled his hand away, Jim saw what Adolfa had seen. Though most of the map was written in unfamiliar, almost runic, symbols, there was one spot that said clearly "**FIRST STOP**." And even better, it seemed like every single color line, every single route, ran through that spot at some point.

Olik grinned. "So there is first stop. We just have to make it there, yes?" He punched Jim on the shoulder, then squeezed Adolfa's arm. "*Bien, abuelita. Muy bien.*"

"No, no," Adolfa waved off his praise, though she was grinning. "You only saw part." She pointed at an area of the map just to the left of where everyone had been looking. "Look."

Jim did. And this time he saw it. It was subtle, especially in the dark. But he saw it.

One of the colored route lines was dark red, perhaps purple. Hard to tell in the dim subway car. But it seemed to pulse in the streaking outside lights, like a living artery with dark blood still pumping through it.

And there, less than an inch away from the location marked **FIRST STOP**, was something else. A small dot, like a clot pushing against the walls of the artery.

And it was moving.

"What does that mean?" Karen's words had more emotion in them than they usually did. Interest, curiosity... and something else. Jim heard her proclaiming "*And they lied!*" and wondered how close to the edge of madness Karen might be dancing. Perhaps she had already fallen into that chasm, and was just reaching for the rest of them, hoping to drag them in with her.

"I think...." Adolfa gulped. She couldn't finish.

"It means we're going to get off!" Olik practically screamed it. He started to laugh. A moment later, so did Adolfa. Jim felt himself begin chuckling as well, and a moment later was clutching at his sides, full-bodied laughter gripping him and rocking him back and forth in waves that were almost debilitating in their strength.

We are mad. Gone crazy, insane over the possibility that a dot on the wall is us, that we might be coming to the end of this horrible trip.

But he couldn't stop. None of them could. And it was totally understandable. Horror and humor were two sides of the same coin. There was a reason why so many horror movies had funny scenes, and why so many comedies were really about quite horrific events. At their base, they were the same. Humor was just terror separated by distance or time; sometimes laughter was what you did when it wasn't socially acceptable to scream.

Only Karen didn't laugh. And that sent a chill down Jim's back.

(*"And they lied!"*)

What was her deal?

The train lurched. Not hard enough to send anyone stumbling forward, but enough that it registered.

"What was that?" asked Karen.

The answer was obvious an instant later.

"We're slowing down," Adolfa managed to say. Her laughter subsided, replaced by glee. "We're stopping."

"First Stop," said Jim, a grin as wide as the old lady's stretching his own face. It felt like he hadn't smiled in an eternity.

169

*(and another thought – but if this is **FIRST STOP** then where is the next one and who gets off there? – broke through his laughter for an instant but he pushed it away with thoughts of Carolyn and Maddie and the smell of their skin and their arms in his)*

Olik laughed so hard he started to cough. He had to pound at his own chest, bending double before he could stop. "Is all fine," he said. "All fine, yes?"

"So it would seem," said Jim.

Because it *was* fine. The lights were going by outside the windows, but they were the normal maintenance lights that Jim had seen on his daily commute for years. They weren't going by so fast they were nothing but laser-like streamers, either. They were just passing at normal, manageable speeds. And instead of hanging in what seemed like total blackness, Jim could see they were on the concrete walls and metal pipes that were typical of New York subway tunnels.

Adolfa leaned forward, bracing herself on the seats so she could look out the window, craning her head to see what lay ahead on the tracks.

Only Karen didn't seem happy. She clutched her satchel, which was still open a crack. Darkness inside the bag, blacker than anything in the train.

The darkness seemed to shake the mirth free of Jim's soul. Adolfa and Olik were still giggling, still laughing to themselves as they looked out the windows. But Jim didn't feel like laughing anymore. He felt... *wrong*. All this was wrong.

"This doesn't make any sense." A strange cloud seemed to have fallen over his mind. He felt muddled.

Drugged. Hadn't he been thinking about drugs a little while ago? Hadn't he been wondering if maybe this was some government experiment on them? Maybe it was. Maybe. Maybe, maybe maybe maybemaybemaybemaybe*maybe*....

He shook his head. *Focus.*

"How did everything back there happen?" he said, jerking a thumb over his shoulder at the door between this car and the last one, the one where Xavier had died. If he *had* died.

Then his motion froze. Because when he looked behind him he saw the door. But beyond it was only the darkness of the tunnel. No car. No trace of the car where Xavier had been mangled from within, no hint of the car beyond *that* one where Freddy the Perv had been flayed to a bloodstain.

As far as Jim could tell, they were once again in the last car on the tracks.

"Guys," he said.

Neither Olik nor Karen took any notice of him. Olik was pumping his good arm manically. His eyes were glassy, like he was only half-aware of what was going on around him. As for Karen, she was looking back and forth between Olik and Jim. Her gaze was the opposite of the big man's: hyper-aware and calculating, as though she was performing a complex mental feat. She didn't look at Adolfa.

"Everyone!" shouted Adolfa, gesturing for the others to come to her window.

"This doesn't make any sense," Jim said to himself.

No one listened. Olik moved to the window the old lady stood at.

"Never thought I would say such a thing," chortled Olik, "but thank God for the New York pigs."

Jim was still shaking his head in confusion, but he felt himself moving as if on autopilot, joining Adolfa and Olik at the window. He peered out and could just see that they were coming up on a subway platform. And that there were flashing lights and groups of men that could only be cops there.

Karen finally joined them. Still clutching the leather case in her red-stained hands. Hands that had been dyed by the blood that flowed from her tablet computer, from the whispering faces of the dead that had appeared there when all this started, when this nightmare ride began.

Olik was still looking out the window. "God bless America and the NYPD, yes?"

"Yes, *mi hijo*, yes," said Adolfa.

"No."

The voice was quiet. Quiet, but it immediately stopped the mirth. There was a level of desperation in it that cut off the joy in the car as effectively as a machete slashing a throat.

Everyone at the window turned to look at the person who had spoken. Karen. She had backed away from the rest of them, moving into the center of the car –

(*the middle car? the back car? which car is this?*)

– where she now stood, still clutching her leather satchel. Her eyes were no longer calm, no longer collected.

They were wild and fever-bright, lit from within by some strange fire that Jim fervently hoped never to understand.

"The cops are here, the cops are here," she said. Olik started to reach into his coat, no doubt going for his gun. "Don't," said Karen. One hand darted into her satchel, then the case fell at her feet like a discarded cocoon. Only what emerged was no butterfly ready to take flight. Instead her hand was clenched around a much deadlier insect – a small black bug with far too few legs and a deadly bite. An insect that Jim recognized from news reports showing terrorists and middle-eastern commandos as a micro-Uzi.

The world seemed to sway under Jim's feet. He expected her to be carrying legal papers in her case, maybe a laptop, even a personal *vibrator* would have been less of a shock to see pulled out of the case right now.

"I knew you were ass-kicker," said Olik. Admiration was unmistakable in his voice as he eased his hand away from his own weapon.

"I thought you were a lawyer," said Jim. The words sounded lame even to him, but he couldn't stop them from coming out. He had to know. There was so much that he didn't understand, and he just had to know *something*, dammit. *Anything.*

"I said I was in *acquisitions*," answered Karen. "And this is the only chance I'm going to have to acquire my contract."

Olik shook his head. He looked resigned, and stepped forward. Karen's gun immediately trained on him. "Always I knew this day would come," he said. "Men like me do not die in bed. Make it quick."

Karen laughed, a quick burst of mirthless noise that punched out of her like a bullet from her gun. "I'm not here for you," Karen said. The micro-Uzi adjusted its aim a half-inch. "Come on, Adolfa."

Jim's lower jaw felt like it was probably going to bounce off his toes. Even more so when the old lady didn't shrink away or even seem particularly surprised. "Now? With the police right outside?"

"You and I know that this is the only time I'll have. After this you'll just disappear again. I don't have time to wait."

"May I say a prayer?" asked Adolfa.

"No."

Karen's finger whitened on the trigger.

And in the same instant, Adolfa ripped in half.

FIVE

Karen pulled the trigger on her micro-Uzi, and at the same moment the lights in the subway tunnel all extinguished. The darkness enveloped them instantly, broken only by the sputter-flare of the automatic weapon as it spat out its deadly payload.

Jim barely noticed. He was too busy trying to sort out what he had just seen.

Adolfa. Torn in two.

At first he thought that it must be something like what had happened to Freddy. Then he replayed what he had seen and realized that was wrong. She wasn't really being pulled apart. Rather, she had split in *two*. Two exact duplicates of the old *latina*. One of them remained in place, and the other leaped to the side with the athletic ability of a circus acrobat.

Jim knew instantly that the standing Adolfa was – *had* to be – the real one. He darted forward and grabbed her. Pulled her back as Karen's tiny weapon continued to stitch strobe flashes in the darkness of the subway car.

Karen was screaming. Madness in her eyes. Madness and something else. Terror? That was part of it, Jim thought. But there was something else, too. Something he didn't understand – and perhaps didn't *want* to understand.

Whatever it was, she didn't seem to notice the Adolfa that Jim had grabbed, the one he had pulled back and who now almost sat atop him as they huddled together off to the side of the car. She was fixated instead on the other Adolfa, the impossibly lithe and gymnastic old lady who was swinging from hand straps and metal bars like an Olympian.

Karen swung her gun in a tight arc, following the old woman around the car. The sputtering shots illuminated everything in stop-gap flashes. It made the lithe Adolfa seem impossibly fast. Here one moment, then in the next flash she was somehow five feet away. The next flash, another five feet away. And in the next....

"I do not see this," whispered Olik.

The impostor Adolfa leaped up in the flash of another missed shot. Leaped up, but not the mere few inches or even the foot she might have done. She jumped all the way to the roof of the car, and there she clung like a huge arachnid. As though the laws of gravity held no sway over her.

Karen was still screaming. Still shooting.

The other-Adolfa scuttled across the roof. Dodging shots. Hissing. Her mouth opened, and Jim saw that the old woman's jaw extended impossibly far, accommodating triple rows of needle-like teeth on both the top and bottom.

Karen's scream elevated.

Under the scream, another sound. A whine. The shriek of brakes.

The subway was slowing.

Stopping.

The Adolfa-thing moved like a lizard. Its jaws clicked shut. It hissed, and the sound was otherworldly, the hiss of something that should never have been seen by earthly eyes.

Click.

The magazine of Karen's weapon was dry. She kept pulling the trigger, kept screaming and pulling the trigger, but nothing happened. Just that dry *click click click*.

The toothy thing that had somehow assumed Adolfa's form dropped from the ceiling. Jim saw that its hands had become hooked claws with lengthy talons. It reached out and yanked the micro-Uzi from Karen's hands with such force that several of the once-beautiful woman's fingers came away as well, yanked off at the knuckles with wet pops that bounced horribly through the subway car.

Karen's scream took on a wet, agonized quality.

The train stopped.

The doors opened.

The platform outside, lit brilliantly before, was now dark.

Karen turned to the now-open doorway. "Help!" she screamed out at the dark platform. She must have decided that whatever she had been paid to "acquire" Adolfa wasn't worth it. "Save us! Save –"

Her voice cut off. It ended so surely and so suddenly that Jim thought the Adolfa-thing must have killed her. It must have plunged one of those dagger-talons into her back and just pulled out her heart.

But no. Karen was still breathing, he saw. Still looking around in the darkness with those fever-spotted eyes, those eyes rimmed with madness and fear.

What was she seeing?

Jim turned. Looked at what Karen was looking at.

He saw that the platform was still full. Not cops after all. But he *did* recognize them. Because he'd seen them all. Seen them very recently, in fact.

A swollen, drowned-looking face.

A woman with a bullet-hole in her forehead.

A man whose tongue had been yanked out, another whose tongue and lower jaw had been abraded away to nothing with a belt sander.

Gunshot wounds, knife wounds, men and women hung and cut and slashed and burned and maimed.

They stood silently on the platform, looking through the subway car's windows, just as they had looked through the glass of Karen's tablet. The faces of the dead.

And at the middle of the platform, standing in front of the open doors… a child. Tiny. No more than five or six. So young it wasn't clear whether it was a boy or a girl. Beautiful. Angelic. And very dead.

Then, as had happened on the tablet screen, the child's features started to melt. To sag. It stepped into the car on legs that were wobbly, loose as though they were made of rubber and skin alone and held no bone within them.

It pointed a drooping finger at Karen.

Karen screamed. The scream muted when the impostor Adolfa swiped out a hand. Karen's throat became a bloody mass. The Adolfa-thing crushed something in her hand, something Jim suspected was Karen's larynx. Then another swipe, and Karen's lower jaw was pulled away in a single piece. Her tongue, no longer enclosed by a mouth, drooped freely against the mangled remains of her neck.

The child at the door to the train pointed again.

"You," it whispered. Its voice bubbled, like its lungs and throat were melting as it spoke.

The Adolfa-thing grabbed Karen by her upper jaw. Jim cringed, sure the thing was going to pull the woman's head apart this time. But it didn't. It flicked the brunette over her back like a grotesque, twitching knapsack.

Karen wasn't screaming anymore. She wasn't even breathing, as far as Jim could see. But she was alive, he knew. Whatever was happening didn't obey the rules of life and death as they knew them. Karen was still alive, still looking around with eyes that were insane and terrified and....

What?

There was that other thing in her eyes, that third thing. A thing he felt like he had to figure out.

Then she was gone. The Adolfa-thing smiled as it passed, triple rows of teeth creating a terrifying depth to its grin, and then it left the subway car. It reached down with its free hand as it passed the melting child. It patted the child's head.

The child's head *blatted*, like a wet and rotten fruit that had been stepped on after being left out too long in the sun.

The Adolfa-thing pulled her hand free, and the child's head came off its body.

Olik said something in his native language that was half scream, half whisper. Jim didn't understand the word, but he understood the terror behind it. He was feeling it, too.

The child's body didn't fall. It just stood there as its head rolled around in the Adolfa-thing's grasp like putty, becoming more and more amorphous, and then finally it had lost all shape or trace of identity. It merged with the Adolfa impostor's own flesh and disappeared.

The child's body, now headless, ran up Karen's form. Scaling her like a decapitated mountain climber, it clambered up her ankles, her legs, her pelvis and stomach and breasts. It climbed to her raw, perforated neck.

Karen couldn't speak. Couldn't make the words, Jim knew. But she started making noise as the headless child made its way up her frame.

"Ung-ung-ung."

Jim felt shivers writhe up his spine, as though shadowing the shivering ascent of the tiny form on Karen's body. The woman was still held in place by the hooked talon of Adolfa's doppelganger, the claw that went through her upper jaw like a hook through a fish.

"Ung-ung-ung."

Karen was making the same sounds Freddy had made.

The headless child, the beast masquerading as a child that should be dead and cold and motionless but somehow was not, plunged its neck toward Karen's face.

And as it did, the rest of the corpses on the platform moved toward her. They closed in on her in a ring, each of them reaching out a hand. The ones that were too far to touch her pulled off bits of their bodies: ears, fingers, noses. They threw the pieces of themselves at Karen, and soon her mutilated body was covered in bloody pieces of the already-dead.

She was still making that noise. That terrible noise. *"Ung-ung-ung."* It was worse than a scream. Screams were what you did when you still had strength, your body's way of saying, *Please save me.* This thing Karen was doing was different. No hope for salvation. Only a quiet pleading for death. For oblivion. *Please kill me. Destroy me.* End *me.*

The child-thing touched its neck to Karen. She started coughing. Blood poured from her nose. Her eyes. Just a bit at first, and then more and more. The blood became a flooding river, a torrent that covered the headless body hunched on her. So much it should have killed her.

But she was still alive. Her eyes still aware.

Her body started to shrivel. Like an apricot left out too long on a summer day. Her skin wrinkled, aged. Her eyes remained bright, but the skin that had been so lovely only a moment before now mottled, then spotted, then crinkled, then cracked. The expensive clothing she had been wearing grew loose and then fluttered free.

Karen was nude, her form a grotesque parody of mummification. But where the ancients had mummified their dead to show them honor and prepare them for safe trips in the afterlife, Jim suspected that this had no such purpose. No, the things masquerading as the dead around Karen were interested in her pain. He could see it in the way they moved, in the way they swayed as if in a trance. They seemed linked to Karen's suffering.

"For the love of God," whispered Adolfa. "Can't someone stop it?"

No one moved.

Karen's figure withered still further. She became nothing more than stick-like bones wrapped in parchment-skin, yellow and dusty. The things around her sighed.

But Karen was still alive. Making that terror/pain/knowing noise. That mad noise. That noise of... something that Jim didn't understand.

For some reason, he thought of the fight with Carolyn. He didn't want a fight to be the last thing she remembered of him.

The things around Karen sighed. They seemed to start melting, their forms growing amorphous. Their limbs drooped like waxen figures too close to a fire. Then their bodies fell into one another, pooling. There was only the headless child-thing on Karen's shriveled, living corpse. Everything else, all the other dead creatures had become a primordial ooze, a thrashing pool of gelatin.

The child-thing reached down with one hand. It touched the horrid pool that writhed all around the platform. The blob oozed up the child's arm. Covered it. Covered the child's body. Then covered Karen's body as well.

"Ung-ung-ung."

The sound she was making disappeared as she was enveloped in the grotesque substance that was all that was left of the dead. Cocooned in decay, a chrysalid wrapped forever in the festering remains of the things that had once been dead and now were something beyond death, something worse. Something dead but alive, dead but hungry.

The doors to the subway shut.

The subway lurched into motion. Carrying Jim and Olik and Adolfa away from the platform, from the sound, from Karen.

The platform dropped back. Soon, mercifully, it was lost in the darkness.

And the subway continued on.

3 FARES

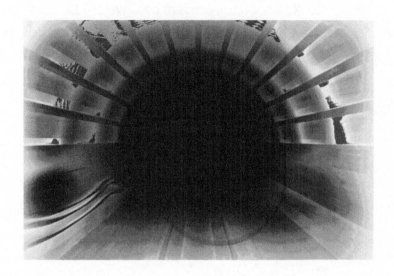

We love to go on picnics. I work a lot at the office – the practice has finally started picking up – so it's rare that we get to do so, but when we can we spread out a feast. Maddie picks what we eat, which means there are a lot of crackers and chips and sugared cereal and it usually ends with upset tummies – mine often the first one.

But I love it. The park is bright and lovely. It's like nothing can go wrong there.

ONE

════════════

════════════

The lights didn't return. Not the ones outside the subway car, and certainly none inside the traveling coffin. Darkness ruled, and light was but a memory.

The three remaining passengers stood frozen in the black for a long time. Jim stared out the windows of the closed doors for what could have been hours, as though if he waited long enough he might have a chance at piercing not only the darkness outside but the darkness that had fallen around his mind. Hopelessness.

He finally turned away, making his way to a seat by touch. He couldn't see anything. Couldn't feel anything, either, beyond an acute sense of how unfair this all was. What had he ever done to deserve this? Why was he here? Where the hell *was* here?

"What do you think is going on?" whispered Adolfa.

Jim started. He hadn't heard her creeping closer. Now, though, he heard the low rustle of her clothing as she sat near to him.

"I don't know," he said. He whispered as well. He didn't know why he felt compelled to do so, but he couldn't deny that he felt like speaking too loud right now would be some kind of a sin. He wasn't much of a church-goer – he was too much a man of science and rationality to spend much time on things like that – but he couldn't deny he felt

186

weirdly like he was sitting in a sanctuary or a confessional right now. "What do you think is happening?"

"*Ay, mi hijo*," she said. "I don't know."

"That lady – Karen."

"Yes?"

"She wanted to kill you."

"She didn't, though."

"No. But why did she want to in the first place?"

He could feel Adolfa's shrug even in the darkness. Or maybe it was just his imagination, giving him something to hold onto so that he didn't go mad from the lack of sensory input. "I dunno," she said. "Crazy lady."

Jim was silent for a moment. There was no question that Karen had been crazy. Sane people didn't walk around New York subways with micro-Uzis in leather cases waiting for opportune moments to gun down old ladies. And yet....

"I guess," he finally said.

"But I don't think the crazy lady is our big problem," added Adolfa.

On that point there was no doubt.

"What's going *on*?" Jim said. He knew he'd already said that, but he couldn't help asking again. As if by repetition he might force Adolfa to provide some hint of information she had withheld until now. Like a child who says, "Please? Please? *Pleeeeeeease*?" knowing it's that last, drawn-out word that will break a parent's defenses.

How much of life is like that? he wondered briefly. How often do we just do the same thing over and over, hoping to get lucky and end up with the outcome we want? Some people said insanity was doing the same thing over and over and hoping for a different result, but wasn't that what we did all the time as a species? Just swinging from the trees and collecting fruit and hoping that one of us lucked out and mutated enough to climb down and start building cities? Where of course we obsessed about constructing the tallest buildings so we could climb back up to the heights we had just abandoned by jumping down from the trees.

I suppose we're *all* a bit insane, he thought.

"I don't know," said Adolfa. She didn't sound angry at having to answer the same question twice. Jim liked her even more for that. She was almost an archetypical grandmother-type. The kind of woman who would always have cookies waiting for you when you visited, who would always have a hug when you needed one.

Unfortunately, he didn't need cookies or a hug now. He needed answers. He needed to get back to his girls.

More noises, heavy and solid thumps on the flooring, announced the arrival of Olik. "I join you, yes?"

"Sure." Jim didn't like the guy. Didn't like what he was, his profession – if you could call it that – but he could hardly deny the man access to this part of the car. What was he going to do, say, "No this part's off limits, go find your own subway car that denies the laws of the universe to sit in"?

Olik sat down somewhere in the darkness nearby.

"So we have lost one more?"

Though phrased as such, Jim could tell it wasn't really a question. Neither he nor Adolfa replied. Silence stretched out between the three of them. It grew uncomfortable, but Jim didn't want to be the one to break it. He just wanted all this to be over. He thought again about just sitting down and waiting. Waiting either for all this to end of its own accord – for someone to come and rescue them – or for some*thing* to come and finish him off. It was an ever-more appealing concept.

Only the phantom scent of Carolyn's hair in his nostrils, the soft touch of Maddie's skin on his fingers, kept him from just sinking into a comatose oblivion. His girls. They needed him. He needed them, too. That was what made a family.

He forced himself to sit up taller. "We've got to get out of here," he said.

"Good," said Olik. "I like to hear this. The sound of fight. You have ideas, Mr. Doctor?"

Jim didn't. "Not a thing. What about you, Adolfa?"

"*Nada, mi hijo.*"

Jim cursed. He felt himself grow angry, and fanned the ember of the emotion until it was a fire. Anger was better than despair. He could use his rage, could make it fuel his actions, push him forward like the flames in a steam locomotive.

He snapped his fingers. "That's it."

"What is it?"

"We've got to stop the train."

Olik guffawed. "This is excellent plan, Mr. Doctor. We just put down feet and stop, yes?"

"No, I mean we have to get outside it. Stop it from the outside." Jim sighed, his frustration becoming palpable. "The subway's powered by electricity. A third rail runs alongside the two track rails, and that rail's the one that provides the electricity to the motor under the train."

"Yes, yes," said Olik. Strange to hear the big man's voice coming from the dark. It was like having a conversation with a ghost. "Electricity in rail, rail touches contact which leads to train. So?"

"So we've got to find the contact point and see if we can break it. That would stop the train, right?"

"Is correct, but...." Olik sighed. "Problems are these: first, how do we do this; and second, what is to say there are not worse things waiting for us outside of stopped train?"

Jim's hands tightened into fists. "I don't know. I don't know the answer to either of those questions. But we have to try *something*, dammit."

"He's right," Adolfa said. "We do have to try something. We can't just wait here to die."

"No, I suppose not."

Something creaked. Then a moment later, Olik's voice sounded from the darkness, closer to the front of the car. "Well? Come then."

Jim got up. It was dark. They were all in the dark.

But they had to get out of this place.

I'm coming, girls.

TWO

=====
=====

Walking forward in a completely dark subway car while it rocketed along at speeds beyond belief turned out to be harder than it sounded. And it sounded pretty hard to begin with. Jim kept rocking to the side, teetering to the ball of one foot, then sliding to the ball of the other foot like a first-time drunk after a world-class bender. He listened for Olik, sure that the big man would have trouble, too, but the Georgian's *tramp tramp tramp* was steady and sure. He might as well have been walking through a well-lit room in his own house.

Behind him, Adolfa was breathing heavily but other than that he couldn't tell if she was having trouble or not. He reached for her but couldn't seem to find her in the darkness.

He bumped into something. Something large and firm and unyielding. It grunted.

"Easy, Mr. Doctor," said Olik.

"Sorry," said Jim. A second later Adolfa bumped into *him* from behind, and that led him to bump into Olik again. This time the grunt the big man coughed out sounded decidedly irritated.

"What now?" said Jim.

"Check door. Feel if will open."

Jim moved up close to Olik. His fingers reached out until they scraped cold metal, then he felt until the seam between door and bulkhead rose up under his fingers. He began feeling along the seam, touching the door and the wall of the subway car on either side, feeling for levers, for knobs. Anything that would let them move to the next car, or at least get out of this one. Adolfa didn't move from behind them. She seemed to know that there was no room for her, that Jim and Olik would take care of this part of things.

"I am thinking what happened to us," said Olik.

"Yeah?"

"I am thinking of *Ourang Medan*."

"Who's that? A," Jim coughed delicately, "*business* partner of yours?"

"No, no. Is not partner. Is boat."

"A boat?" Jim was moving slowly. Only halfway up the seam. He didn't want to miss anything. He had heard that when you lost your sight your other senses became sharper, but if that was the case it must be a gradual thing because he felt like he was losing his sense of touch as well. He moved his fingers even slower.

"A ship. A haunted ship."

Jim couldn't restrain the quick laugh that belted out. "You don't strike me as the type that believes in ghosts, Olik."

"Nor am I type who believes in men who go *poof* into pile of blood and coat, or man who has baby crawl from mouth, or woman who...." He trailed off. No need to finish. They had all seen it.

"You think this subway is haunted?" Adolfa's voice was tremulous. That she believed in ghosts was not a surprise. She was probably crossing herself again, Jim thought. Saying a quick prayer to some saint, asking for protection from whatever angelic person was in charge of underground tunnels and insane subways.

"Perhaps."

"What we've seen didn't look like ghosts," said Jim. He felt something on the bulkhead and his heart skipped. Then he realized it was just another seam in the metal. Rivets under his fingers where two sheets of steel came together. He continued tracing the wall and door.

"On *Ourang Medan*, the sailors perhaps never see ghosts either. But when they were found by American ships, it looked for certain they had gone mad."

"We're not going mad."

"Aren't we?" Olik grunted. Sounded like he was pulling on something. "How else you explain this all?" Another grunt. The door rattled but didn't move. "We are neck-*deep* in madness, Mr. Doctor."

"What happened to them?" said Adolfa. "To the sailors on the boat?"

Olik didn't answer for a moment. There was a click, and the door started to slide back. But any hope that might have been found in the door's movement was quashed by his next words.

"They died. All of them."

THREE

The door slid open, and Jim was surprised when Olik didn't step out. Then he realized the big Georgian was waiting for Jim to precede him. At first he thought the man was trying to get him to risk his neck in case something was waiting out in the space between cars, and almost stood his ground. Then he moved forward. Partly that was because he realized that they were as likely to be killed where they stood as anywhere. And partly it was because he didn't think Olik was treating him as a guinea pig in this instance. No, he felt almost like the other man was saying, "It was your idea to get out here, so let's see what you do."

Any hopes that Jim might have had of stopping the train from the outside were dashed when he stepped onto the platform between cars. Unlike the space between the previous cars, there was no covering to shield the platform from the tunnel. Here, the platform that hung like a suspension bridge between the car they were on and the next one was open to the tunnel, open to the world outside the train... whatever world that might be. Jim could feel the air whipping past, could hear the unblocked echo of the train's passing on the tunnel walls.

But within seconds he knew there was no hope of getting to the third rail or the subway's motor or any contact points between them. It was just as dark out here as it had been in the car, and any attempt to fiddle with the mechanisms underneath or outside the subway car would equate to passive-aggressive suicide attempts. He would fall, he would be sucked under the train, he would be mangled by the wheels, he would be maimed by passing machinery. The possibilities were endless, and the only thing they all had in common was that they all ended badly for him.

"I can't see shit out here," said Jim. It was more a declaration of frustration than an informational statement, just something to say in order to let the others know that he couldn't do anything, and the anger he felt welling up about that fact.

Adolfa *tsk-tsk*ed quietly from the car behind him. Grandmothers everywhere would prefer that cursing be kept at a minimum, apparently. Even when faced with horrible, impossible death, please keep a civil tongue.

Jim hated her in that moment. He was a grown man. He had been dressing himself for years. He had even seen an R-rated movie or two. He could curse if he felt like it. For a second he thought about turning around and calmly saying each curse word he knew. Not yelling it, just sort of listing them off. To see how she would react.

Instead he felt his way out onto the platform. There were guardrails on the outsides of the platform, presumably to keep people from pitching off the narrow shelf and into dark oblivion – wouldn't want anyone to fall and miss their chance to be dissolved or impregnated with a miniature version of themselves or otherwise horribly dispatched. In spite of the irony of the guardrails, though, Jim put a hand on each as he edged into the nothing that separated the cars.

What if it *is* nothing? he thought. What if there's nothing past the platform?

A horrible image entered his mind, a vision of himself putting a foot down in the darkness, only there was nothing there to put it on. The platform ended, there was no connecting car. Nothing before or behind this car, it was just a singularity in the void that the universe had become. And Jim fell off the platform, not to be crushed under the car's wheels, but simply to fall forever, falling and falling and falling and falling. He saw himself screaming until he could scream no more, losing himself in a madness that was truly all-encompassing, because the universe would have cast itself away, and all that would be *left* was madness.

He put his feet down more carefully after that.

After only a few more steps his toe nudged something hard. The door to the next car. He let go of one of the guardrails. His entire body clenched when he did it, as though he was letting go of one of one of his few remaining tethers to reality.

"You okay, Doctor Jim?"

Jim almost jumped right off the platform. "Fine," he snapped. "Shut up."

Silence from behind. He felt forward. Found the car with his blindly groping hand. He miscalculated the distance slightly and his fingers bashed the steel door, crumpling against it. He barked in pain.

"You –" began Adolfa.

"Shhh," hissed Olik. "Doctor Jim said no to bother him."

"I don't care." Adolfa sounded petulantly resolute. Jim could imagine her stamping her tiny foot as she stood up to the giant man. "He could be hurt."

Jim decided to forestall the argument. "I'm okay," he shouted.

"You see?" said Olik. "The doctor is fine, yes?"

It would have been a comical interplay in any other situation. Even now, Jim felt the urge to smile. He didn't let himself do it, though. He felt like that would be wrong somehow. This was not a place to smile. This was a serious place.

His hand found a strip of metal. A crash bar. He hesitated for a moment when he found it. Was this kind of latch normal on a subway car? He couldn't remember. He was a long-time subway commuter, the kind of guy who knew how to get anywhere in New York with the right subway token, ticket, or card. But he couldn't remember if this was how subway cars felt, if this was the kind of latch they had on their doors.

Maybe Olik's right, he thought. Maybe we're all nuts.

But that was another dead end. If he was insane, sitting in a padded cell and drooling his way to the next meal time or making *papier mâché* art using blunt scissors, then there was nothing he could do. There was no escape, no way out of this.

And he had to get out of this. He had always gotten out of every bad situation. Every time. Even when his mother had –

(*been murdered hacked to pieces blood everywhere all over the walls all over her sheets all over her eyes her open eyeballs and pooling on her open eyes so much blood*)

– even with what had happened with her, even then he had found a way to rise above it. To turn difficulty into triumph and the promise of a better tomorrow.

Jim pushed the crash bar. He didn't really expect it to depress, and even if it did he didn't expect the door to the next car to open.

But the crash bar *did* depress. The door *did* open.

"The next car's open," he called back. Immediately he heard movement behind: Olik and Adolfa must have been eager to get out of the car, out of the moving headstone.

He stepped forward.

FOUR

It was just as dark in the new car as it had been in the old. But Jim still felt better here. They were moving forward. That was progress, wasn't it? Sooner or later they would have to get to the front of the subway train, and then they could...

... what?

Jim thought about the driver he had seen earlier, the man with the too-gaunt face, beckoning him forward. Did he expect they would be able to just chat with that cadaverous looking fellow, simply ask the guy to pull over and let them off somewhere uptown?

Jim doubted it would be that simple. But that didn't mean he was going to stop moving forward.

Of course, the driver could want you to do just that.

The thought was hardly welcome. What if they were being herded somehow? Led like calves down a chute where a butcher would be waiting with a bolt stunner, ready to pound their brains with a piston that would turn their gray matter into jelly.

Something touched Jim's back. His skin felt for a moment as though it was trying to crawl off his bones, or as though it had suddenly shrunk several sizes.

"Is that you, Doctor Jim?" Olik's voice managed to both boom and whisper at the same time, and Jim's skin returned to something approaching normalcy as he realized it was the big man's hand on his back.

"Yeah. Is Adolfa with you?"

"Right here, *mi hijo.*"

Jim pressed slowly forward, Olik's hand a constant pressure on his back. "What does *mi hijo* mean, anyway?" he whispered. He was talking to talk, trying to fill the void with something warm, something real.

"It means 'my son.'"

That was nice. Not nice enough to offset the distinctly *un*niceness of walking through the darkness like this, but nice nonetheless.

He pushed forward an inch at a time, hands outstretched and waving before him. He fully expected to come into contact with something grotesque at any moment. To touch scales or horns or talons or something worse for which humanity had no name. But there was nothing. Just air.

The walk seemed to last forever. Jim felt like he was trekking across a dark galaxy, a distance measured not in feet or even miles but in light-years.

"Olik," he said. He had to speak. The silence and darkness were overwhelming him. Driving him crazy. He was starting to see flashes, but they weren't real. Just jelly-blobs of light that existed only in his mind. They looked like blood. Like bloody sheets. Eye sockets pooling with red.

"Yes, Doctor Jim."

"What happened to that ship? The *Oura....*"

"The *Ourang Medan*? It was Dutch ship. American ships were sent message from ship, message that said 'Come aboard. All officers and captain dead.' And then another message: 'I die.' They came aboard and found all men dead. And then...."

Silence. "Then?" said Adolfa. Jim took another step into darkness. How far did this car extend? He was sure it should have ended; sure they should have reached the front by now. It felt like like he'd been walking for years.

"The Americans leave. They ran. Some say is because there was a fire and they had to get out. But I think is because they knew if they stayed, they would be caught, too. So they left. They ran, and blew up the *Ourang Medan* before its spirits could capture them as well. Before they could be trapped by madness, and death could come for them."

The hand on Jim's back trembled. Jim stopped moving forward. "You okay, Olik?" he said.

"Fine."

Jim shook his head in the darkness. "Bull."

"Just tired. Hand hurting a bit."

"Sit down."

"Would rather keep moving."

"And I'd rather not have to carry you the rest of the way."

"You will never carry me. I guarantee that." The pride was easy to hear in Olik's voice. Even so, Jim heard the big man sit down on something. Jim sat, too, and was surprised to find that the seats were different again.

Neither the new seats that had been in the last car, nor the older seats in the one before. No, these felt plush. Regal.

"Comfy," said Adolfa.

"Yeah." Jim closed his eyes. He would not have thought it possible, but he felt suddenly sleepy. He wanted to curl up for a nap.

Then sleep fled as something flashed. A light. Not outside the car, either. This was a light within the metal box that he had come to despise so very much. A snapping, flaring brightness as the lights in the subway car all went on at once.

They extinguished almost as fast as they came. Just an instant. A single moment in what had come to seem like an eternity of darkness. But it was enough.

Their current subway car was old. Even older than the one they had just left. It looked like maybe one of the first subway cars to have been built, all leather and wood and glass and subtly rough edges that bespoke hand-tooling. There were benches covered in thick padding, and every few feet the benches broke and a pair of Victorian-style four-legged chairs sat bolted to the floor. It almost looked like an old-fashioned Pullman carriage.

The flashing lights came from kerosene lamps bolted above every third window. They flickered with living flame, though they had all come on at the same exact moment, and had all turned off at the same time as well.

Jim also noted that, in the hours – it had seemed like *days* – that they had been inching forward – they had only managed to move up the car about ten feet.

The lights went out with an audible snap.

"What now?" said Olik. The big man sounded weary. Jim wondered how much longer he would last. And what would happen if he lost so much blood that he could no longer walk.

The darkness had seemed profound before. This time, with the memory of light burning behind his eyes, Jim found it oppressive. It had a physical weight, pressing down on him like water in the ocean depths. He felt like he might be crushed by it.

I can't do this. I can't do this.

You have to do it. Get to the girls. Get to your girls.

He felt the outline of the small book in his pocket. Pictured the smaller photo folded within it.

Don't give up.

I won't. I promise.

The lights flared into brightness again.

Beside him, Adolfa screamed. Jim didn't blame her. He would have done the same, but his voice had been stolen, completely and utterly, by what he saw all around him.

He had promised himself only a moment ago – less – that he would not give up. And now he wondered if he would be able to keep that promise. The darkness, so heavy, so crushing and devastating only an instant before, now seemed to beckon to him like a memory of happiness with an old friend.

He wished the darkness would return. Because then he wouldn't have to see what was all around him. All around *them*.

"We're going to die," whispered Olik.

Jim nodded. The big man was right.

They were *all* going to die.

FIVE

They were everywhere.

Never in his most crowded travel day had Jim seen a subway car as full as this one was now. He was reminded of stories of the Holocaust: Jews and other "undesirables" packed into railroad cattle cars like diseased livestock and sent off to meet their ends at Dachau or Auschwitz. Those men and women had no choice but to stand, pushed so tightly together that movement was all but impossible.

That was how Jim felt now. Like he had been packed in tighter than a puzzle piece. A jumble in a human game of Tetris.

But he had not been packed into a car with other commuters. Not even with people doomed to a death in the gas chambers or work camps of an invading force.

No, at every turn, within inches of him and Adolfa and Olik... the ghouls. The things that looked like the rotted shells of once-teens, mostly girls, who had perhaps clawed their ways out of shallow graves and were now bent on avenging those who had buried them.

Adolfa was whispering something under her breath. Jim assumed it was a prayer. "Shhh!" he hissed. But she didn't stop. Probably *couldn't* stop.

The lights went out again. Darkness fell once more, blanketing the car in its perfect embrace. But there was no sense of security in that hold. Jim could feel the sway of the things that stood and sat only inches away from him. Could feel the strange cool that emanated from their bodies, the chill of death long overdue. He shivered.

"They have come for me," said Olik. The big man sounded, for the first time, genuinely terrified.

"We don't know that."

"They have! They come for me!" Olik's once-sturdy voice was starting to fray, to come apart at the seams. Jim couldn't figure why the Georgian was so convinced the things were here for him. Then he remembered their snakelike tongues, flicking out and lapping up the big man's blood as it splashed on the door of the subway car.

And Olik was still bleeding.

"We have to get moving," Jim said.

The lights flared again. The effect was strange, like an old-fashioned photo being taken. Only with every pop of the "flash" in this case, they were either one step closer to death, or one step closer to escape.

You can't *escape, Jim. You know that.*

Shut up!

The outline of the book in his pocket. He could feel it against his thigh. The memories, driving him forward. *His* memories. His girls. He would survive for them.

Adolfa was right behind him. He could feel her close to him. Still whispering a prayer in Spanish, strident tones whose rhythm somehow managed to perfectly match the *click-clack click-clack click-clack* of the subway's wheels on its track.

And in the darkness behind Adolfa, Jim thought he could hear Olik. Then he knew he could. He heard the distinctive click of a gun being cocked.

The light flared.

The things were all looking at them. Like they had heard the gun. Were centered on it. *Wanted* it.

"Put it away, Olik," Jim snapped.

"No," said Olik.

The things turned as one. Not just looking at them, now *oriented* on them. On Olik. On the gun.

"Put *it away*."

Olik must have seen what Jim did. There was a clatter of metal on metal. The gun dropping to the floor.

Jim held himself still. Tense. Expecting to feel teeth tear into him, small bodies cover his and fingers dig into his skin and burrow into his bones.

Would he be killed/reborn like Xavier? He didn't think so. Whatever had happened to the rapist, he thought it was something that would only happen once.

The light flared.

The things were looking at the gun.

"Come on." Jim stepped forward as the light died. He tried to keep an image of the front door in his mind. Tried to imagine a line of rope that ran from him to the door, guiding him there unerringly, perfectly. But he knew it wouldn't happen.

He bumped into the first body in only a step. It was as cold as he had imagined it would be. Colder, in fact.

Not the cold of a winter day, not even the cold of a freezer. It was the cold of a morgue, the cold of a place that is designed to pull away the life from something. To leave it dead and hanging like a fly from a spider's web.

He hissed.

"You all right?" Olik's voice. Strained and awkward, though whether because of ongoing blood loss or simple terror Jim couldn't tell.

"Fine." Jim kept pressing forward. Trying to forget the feel of the corpse he had bumped into. Because that was what it was; of that he had no doubt. The things in the car with them were dead. All of them. They might see, they might stand, they might even think on some level. But there was no life in them. No life but what they perhaps hoped to steal back from the living around them.

Jim's outstretched hand touched another one. A bit of cloth, crumbling and rotten under his hand; a span of grisly flesh that reminded him of how the things had attacked one another to get to the blood around them.

The ghoul jerked away. It snarled, but didn't attack. Jim felt dizzy. He almost lost his bearings in the darkness. How could he get through this?

He could get through this the same way people had been doing the impossible for centuries. For his family.

Another step forward. The light flared. *Pop.* The things all around.

Jim could smell them now, too. The smell of rot, like the smell that escaped a rock when you rolled it over and first saw bugs running for cover, afraid because you had discovered them in their secret darkness. Only this putrescence was much stronger, much deeper. A rot that pushed through every molecule of air in the car, that brought with it an almost tangible sense of hopelessness.

The light dimmed. Another step forward.

Pop.

Another step forward. Bumping another ghoul. A girl who had died an hour or a year before, the skin of her face sloughing off in sheets, her eyes clouded with necrotic cataracts, blind yet somehow able to sense the presence of life nearby. The ghoul made a noise startlingly reminiscent of the sounds Freddy the Perv and Karen of "acquisitions" had made in their final moments –

(*Ung-ung-ung... ung-ung-ung....*)

– and then the lights dimmed again.

Jim became aware of panting. He thought at first that it was his own, then realized it was someone else's. Adolfa's? No, she was still praying, still half-chanting in a language he didn't speak but that still was easily understandable as something that boiled down to "Deliver us from Evil."

The panting was coming from Olik.

"Olik, stay calm," he whispered. Then hissed as his outstretched fingers touched something wet and sticky. He didn't know what it was. Didn't want to know. He shuffled to one side. Tried to move around. Concentrated on the imaginary rope that tied him to the door at the front of the subway car.

"Can't." Olik started wheezing. "I need my gun."

Flash. Lights on. And Jim saw Olik turning around. Turning back to where his gun sat on the floor of the car.

"Olik, don't," said Adolfa.

"Don't go," said Jim at the same time. Both spoke under their breath.

The zombie things seemed to take no notice of them. No care. Jim wondered what would set them off, if anything. They had seemed to fixate on the gun. He thought about darting after Olik, grabbing the big man before he could get to his gun. But what was he going to do? It wasn't like he could overpower the huge man.

The lights dimmed.

Flash. Back on. The lights were popping on and off faster now, faster than was possible for a kerosene lamp. It seemed almost like a series of strobe lights hung along the edges of the car.

On, off, on, off, on off on off onoff onoffonoffonoff....

Olik was back with them. Jim sighed in relief. The big man had come to his senses. Had realized that his gun wasn't worth dying for. Or worse.

They were two-thirds of the way down the car.

Jim touched another zombie. This one was wearing a pink skirt. A matching pink tube top. It looked like she was getting ready to go clubbing, or had been before death had claimed her, before rot had set in and eaten out her eyes and lips and ears and nose.

Jim was half-used to the clammy touch of the zombies at this point. Just stay cool, he told himself. Just don't react and you'll be fine.

But this time it was different.

He touched the thing's bare skin, a length of clammy gray-white flesh between the tube top and the skirt. And the thing reacted instantly, throwing herself at him. Her teeth – jagged and far too visible between the lips that had been shredded by death and time – snapped at him. Jim fell back with a cry, colliding with Adolfa. She went down as well, both falling at Olik's feet.

The thing snapped and snarled, her lipless jaws reaching for Jim's face, his flesh, his throat. He pushed at her shoulders with his hands, trying to keep her away from him. She was strong – far stronger than she should have been. And at the same time, her bones seemed able to collapse in on themselves, like they had rotted within her, so there was nothing solid enough for him to grab and get purchase on to push her away.

The lights were still flashing, almost pulsing now. The strobe was giving him a headache. He didn't know if he was going to be able to hold off this girl, this thing.

Then a hand, large and strong, wrapped itself around the girl's throat. It hauled her off Jim, yanking her into the air by the neck like a naughty puppy. It was Olik, his one good hand tearing the ghoul away from Jim and then tossing her behind them into the mass of undead in the car behind.

The ghouls that she collided with fell upon each other in a rage. Teeth and nails, fingers and feet. Howls of pain as thick, dark blood spattered. A contained maelstrom in the center of the car.

"Get up," said Olik. "We go."

Jim pushed to his feet. He took the lead again. Careful now not to touch the ghouls. They were changing, growing more alert, more ready to attack. He hadn't sensed it before, but now he could. There was an electricity in the air, a charge that seemed to make the small hairs on his arms and the back of his neck stand up straight as soldiers at parade rest.

Something's going to happen.

He knew not to touch the ghouls. The lights popped and dimmed, popped and dimmed, and he led the others between the monsters. Holding Adolfa's hand, and she held onto Olik's. A train of the living among all these dead.

The going was slow. So slow, because every time Jim came within inches of the things around them, they snuffled and snorted as though they had caught the scent of something delicious. He moved sideways, around. Up and over, around and down. Sidestepping when necessary, climbing on seats when he had to.

Then he got to a spot where there was nothing. No way forward. He was blocked by a solid wall of the things, an unbroken mass of the undead.

Flash, dark. Flash, dark.

He looked back at Adolfa. She shrugged, her eyes wide. She looked terrified.

Olik was making a motion. Putting his good hand flat, then dipping it down. Jim didn't understand what he was trying to convey, and wanted to tell him to just say whatever it was. But he didn't, because he didn't know if the things around them would be attracted to sound the same as they now seemed to be attracted to touch.

Finally, though, he realized what Olik was trying to tell him. He shook his head. Impossible.

Olik made the same motion. More stridently this time, as though to say, "Do it, dammit."

Flash, dark. Flash, dark.

Jim was getting disconcerted. Losing control of his sense of up and down as well as his emotional control.

He shook his head again. Adolfa's hand moved toward him. For a moment he thought she was going to attack him. He almost punched her, almost hit her in her gently smiling face.

Then her hand fell on his shoulder. Pushed him gently down. She nodded and smiled.

Flash, dark. Flash, dark.

"It's the only way," the old lady seemed to be saying. "Just do what you have to do."

Jim felt the book in his pocket. The square outline that held so many dreams in its pages.

He turned.

There were three ghouls, standing so close that they might as well be one devilish monster with three heads. All three were in various states of dissolution, though all were recognizable as once having been girls in their teens. The rags of once-cute clothes hung from their bony frames, t-shirts with fun logos draping sunken breasts, skirts with pleats and ragged frills hanging below hip bones that poked visibly through the girls' flesh.

One of the girls was taller than the others. She could have been a real beauty when alive, with long legs and the kind of slim body structure that graced modeling magazines the world over. Her legs were planted wide, swaying slightly as the subway continued on its trip to wherever it was going.

Jim looked at her face. One cheek was torn away, the flap hanging against her lower jaw. Her eyes stared sightlessly over him. She wore makeup, a garish amount that made him think of the girls who walked on certain street corners in the less-reputable parts of the city. The makeup was almost the worst thing about her.

Jim felt Adolfa's hand on his shoulder, still pushing. He knelt. Went to hands and knees. He didn't know if he could do this. Didn't know if it was possible physically *or* mentally.

But I'm going to try.

He edged forward, the metal floor cool under his palms.

The ghoul's feet came closer. More than shoulder length apart, they were clad in what must once have been bright yellow high heeled shoes. Something that would attract attention, certainly, in much the same way that her makeup would have attracted attention.

Jim suddenly thought of his mother. She had hated girls like this. Hated them so much.

(*but she doesn't hate anything now. now she's at peace, at peace....*)

The subway rocked for a moment, as though hitting a large seam on the tracks. The ghoul sidestepped. The left foot almost collided with Jim. He managed to roll with the motion, though. Then held himself still, so still that not even a breath escaped him. He could hear Adolfa and Olik, too, both of them inhaling as though to hold their breath in concert with him.

214

He resumed pushing forward. No longer room to crawl. Crawling would inevitably knock him into the legs that now straddled him. All he could do was sort of *worm* his way forward. It took forever. The train rolled and hummed beneath him.

Where the hell are we going?

Then he was through.

He stood. Almost as dangerous as the crawl had been, since there were more dead things on the other side of the ghoul, so close that if he stood wrong he would bump them and trigger what he feared would be a chain reaction, a feeding frenzy.

Then he was standing. Safe.

Flash, dark. Flash, dark.

He caught Adolfa's eye. She nodded. Her face was pale, she looked like she was going to be sick. Jim hoped she could hold back her nausea: he didn't know how the zombies would react to someone vomiting, but he doubted it would be pretty.

Adolfa sunk down out of sight. Jim couldn't do anything but move out of the way. He couldn't even lean over to give her a hand. There wasn't enough room for that.

But Adolfa proved far more agile than her years would seem to allow. She was through the zombie's parted legs and standing beside Jim in less time than it had seemed to take him to traverse the same distance.

Olik was all that remained.

The big man took his place. Jim hoped that there would even be enough room for the huge Georgian to get between the zombie's legs.

Olik sunk out of sight.

And as he did, the zombies – all of them, every single one in the car – sighed. And as had happened before, it was as though one single entity was expressing itself through fifty mouths.

And it sounded hungry.

SIX

Flash, dark. *Flash, dark.*

Jim blinked, his body trying to turn away the assault of light and dark. But it couldn't do it. There was no way to refuse it, no way to resist it. The darkness was too harsh, the light too sudden. The contrast was destructive, and he knew that unless he got out of this car soon he was going to lose his mind.

Adolfa pressed into him. Lost as he was in the strobe patterns of black and white, Jim almost didn't understand what was happening for a moment. Then he realized: Olik must be coming through.

Through? Through what? Through when? Through where?

The world seemed to gyre and whirl, to dance drunkenly.

Only it's not the world, is it? Not really. Because then the world would be nothing but the subway. Nothing but this car, nothing but this metal death.

Adolfa's hand closed on his. "Steady, *mi hijo.*"

Mi hijo. My son.

Jim clung to the words and to the endearment beneath them. Clung to them as much as – more than – he clung to her hand. The world steadied.

217

Flash, dark. Flash, dark.

Olik stood.

"We go," he said. And now he was the one who took point. Jim didn't like that. He wanted to go first. He felt too alone, too exposed at the end of the human train that was being led through the car.

What if he leaves you? Leaves Adolfa? Leaves you both to the wolves?

The voice that came to Jim's mind wasn't exactly his. It sounded like his voice, but it spoke to him as though it was someone else, like a long-lost twin who had traveled through time and space to find him in this instant, to warn him of the danger that Olik represented.

He's a sex-trader. He's a slaver. He's used you before and he'll do it again.

The big man stepped gingerly between two half-dressed girls, dead girls with dead eyes and teeth that were startlingly white in the light/dark of the subway car. He pulled Adolfa with him. The two zombie girls didn't notice either of them. They stared into nothing, into dreams of their demise, perhaps, or the blank nothings of their futures.

Flash, dark. Flash, dark.

Jim stepped between the dead girls. One of them was wearing the decrepit remains of a cheerleader's outfit. The other wore jeans and a tank top. Both stood slump-shouldered, and he somehow knew that their posture had nothing to do with their state of decomposition. It was something that had been done to them in life. It was the *reason* for their death.

Flash, dark. Flash, dark.

The front of the car was only a few feet away. Within reach. Within hope.

Hope was the worst. Jim knew that hope was the thing that allowed fear to thrive. Without hope there was nothing for fear to feed on. But when hope bloomed, that meant that there was once again something to lose. Something to be terrified of living without.

Hope came. Came like the bright flash of the lamps all around the ancient subway car. And on its heels, the dark bite of terror.

"Go, go, *vámonos, vámonos,*" said Adolfa. Her voice, whispered in half-dark, half-light, was so intense that Jim knew without having to look at her face that she was feeling the same dread, the same creeping horror that this was it, the last moment they had before all was extinguished, before the lights went out for the last time.

Something was happening behind them. A rustle as the zombies began to move.

"Don't look," said Jim. "Don't look back."

Adolfa jerked, her head moving as though she *was* going to look, then stopping and forcing herself forward, onward.

The door was close. Would it be open? Unlocked?

Whatever was happening behind them grew more strident. Insistent. It demanded attention.

There were three zombies between Jim, Olik, and Adolfa... and the door out of the car. They stared in different directions, dead to the world. Jim saw Olik eyeing them, obviously determining the best way to thread his way between them without touching them, without drawing the attention of the dead girls. Like the rest of the creatures, they were dressed brightly, almost gaudily. Like the rest of the creatures, their dead eyes gazed at nothing, peered into a void of lost dreams and horrific memories that Jim hoped he would never understand.

Olik stopped suddenly. He stared at one of the ghouls. She was dressed skimpily, a pair of short shorts that showed off thighs whose flesh was peeling away in mottled chunks and a tight tank top that revealed far more than it hid. The kind of thing that Jim hoped Maddie would *never* wear.

If he was even around to *have* that argument with her.

Olik remained riveted to the zombie. He bore a strange expression on his face, one that Jim couldn't place. Then he could place it, but didn't understand it: it was... *familiarity*.

The sounds behind them grew louder. Hisses. Thuds. Jim didn't look back. Didn't *have* to look back to know that the zombies were attacking one another again. He didn't know why they would be doing that, what would motivate them to tear into one another, but that was what had to be happening.

The three ghouls – including the one that Olik seemed to be transfixed by – suddenly shifted their sightless gaze, latching their eyes onto whatever was happening in the back of the car.

Flash, dark. Flash, dark.

Jim worried that the zombies would see him and Olik and Adolfa – would really *see* them. But the three girl-things didn't notice them. They shambled toward the back of the car, and Jim and his companions simply stepped aside and let them move past.

The way to the door was clear.

"Home free," said Jim. He looked at Adolfa. Smiled. She smiled back.

They moved to the door in two quick steps.

Flash, dark. Flash, dark.

The disturbance behind them got louder. Louder.

Jim reached for the door to the car.

Something was shrieking.

Jim's fingers stopped moving, halting as though they had run into an invisible force field.

Flash, dark. Flash, dark.

The shrieking wasn't the inhuman sound of the ghouls. It wasn't any of the inhuman noises they had heard on this longest of trips to nowhere.

It was Olik.

SEVEN

The big man's screams were so raw and ragged that Jim fully expected to turn around and find that Olik had fallen prey to one of the zombies, or that he had been pulled apart like Freddy the Perv had.

But nothing had touched Olik. Nothing at all.

He was standing there in the light/dark/light/dark, screaming and screaming and screaming, and *nothing had touched him*. He was alone.

The big man was staring behind them. Looking back into the car.

Jim followed his gaze. He saw the disturbance. The zombies in the car had all converged on something. Jim couldn't see what it was for a moment, because the things were packed so tightly that not a single photon could have squeezed between them. There was no way to see what they were huddled around.

Then the zombies parted. They stood as if to accommodate Jim's unspoken need to see what was hiding in their midst. They turned, and he thought they were looking at him, then realized they were staring at Olik.

Olik was still screaming.

Jim didn't scream. But he felt his throat suddenly grow parched, as though he had tried to swallow a handful of sand.

There were two girls in the midst of the zombies. Not dead. Alive. Alive, and bright, and terrified. They looked young, perhaps only thirteen or fourteen. Young and horror-stricken as they huddled in the center of the living corpses that encircled them.

Olik was still shrieking, but the wordless scream had morphed to something else: "Nina! Sanatha!"

The two girls in the middle of the circle looked up. They screamed back at him. Fingers reaching for the big man.

Jim felt something tugging at him. It was Adolfa, pulling him back toward the front door. He didn't move. He felt like he had been fastened to the floor, nailed to the spot. He had to watch what was happening. To bear witness.

Olik reached out to the two girls. "Nina!" He stepped toward them, but immediately several of the ghouls moved to intercept him. Jim expected that they would attack him, but they didn't. The zombies just stood between him and the two girls at the center of the car, staring at the big man with eyes that saw nothing of the pain on his face.

The other zombies had watched his approach. Now they turned back to the two girls. The girls were similar in size, but one was blonde and one brunette. They had the same eyes, though. Sisters, Jim guessed. They looked familiar somehow.

They looked, he realized, like beautiful, unhardened versions of Olik.

The zombies surrounded the girls. Sighing in that singular voice, that one voice that came from many throats. And this time it didn't just moan, it spoke. "*Huuuunngryyyyy.*"

The girls screamed. Held each other.

One of the ghouls reached out. Touched the girl with the dark hair.

"Nina!" Olik shouted.

Flash, dark. Flash, dark.

Nina screamed. Screamed louder when the zombie's touch turned into a pinch. Not like it was trying to rip the flesh from her bones, but like it was... *sampling* her. Seeing how tender she was, checking the quality of her body.

And now from the churning mass of monsters, another hand reached out. It touched the other girl. Sanatha. She shouted as well, a high-pitched shriek that was as much surprise as horror. She looked at Olik and babbled something in a foreign tongue.

Jim looked at Olik. The big man reached out, still blocked by the ghouls. He was crying.

A claw-like hand swiped at Sanatha. Raked a bloody furrow in her leg. She screamed and fell. Olik screamed as well. He seemed to go insane, trying to break through the wall of zombies between him and the girls. But they held him back effortlessly. He collapsed, weeping, and they hauled him to his feet. Pulled his hair back so he had to watch.

Nina and Sanatha were yanked, pulled. Clawed, bitten. Soon they were bleeding from dozens of wounds, their clothing in tatters.

Jim saw Olik pull away. Saw him clench his face, trying to shut out the vision that he saw in the flashing light/dark of the car.

One of the ghouls that held Olik reached out – almost delicately – and pulled his eyelids off. The girl-thing flicked the bits of skin away as Olik screamed, blood running around his eye sockets, but he could no longer blink, could no longer look away from the vision of the girls being pulled to pieces in front of him.

One of the ghouls pushed through the circle. Most of the things were girls. Most of them. This one, though, wasn't. It was male, and that fact was easy to be seen. It was nude, and visibly excited by what it saw as it moved into the circle.

"No, no, *no no no!*" screamed Olik. "Not my babies!"

The ghouls paid him no heed. The ones forcing him to watch pulled him toward the circle that surrounded the girls. The ghouls in that circle were no longer clawing at them, they were pulling at their clothes, exposing shivering flesh.

Jim knew what was happening. Knew but couldn't believe, couldn't accept. Not this. Not this.

Olik was screaming.

"Not my babies, not my babies, not my bab*ieeeeezzzzz!*"

Jim felt Adolfa's hand on his arm. Pulling him again. He heard a click and knew that she must have opened the door to the next car.

This car had taken its victim.

Olik was still screaming as Jim let himself be pulled away from the obscenity behind him. The stolid criminal was gone, replaced by a hysterical father who saw his world disappearing, defiled and demeaned. The screams of the girls in the center of the circle matched that of the big man. His voice and theirs' mingled and matched in a horrific harmony that bled into madness. Then, in the moment of greatest savagery, the moment when the worst was happening, the zombies gripping Olik took hold of his shoulders and others took hold of his head and both sets of dead girls yanked.

There was a tearing sound, a shearing rip that tore not just through the air but through Jim's mind, pushing him close to madness as well. Olik's head came away from his shoulders. Flesh and bone and blood sprayed and now Olik was in two pieces, both held upright by the rotted hands that clutched his flesh.

But – impossibly – the man still screamed. Still screamed as his daughters screamed, as they were savaged by things come for them from beyond the darkest reaches of nightmare.

Adolfa's hand pulled Jim's. He let her.

He stepped with her into the darkness of the next car.

Olik's scream followed them.

And the subway continued on.

226

2 FARES

Carolyn wants to move. I love her, but this is the five hundredth time she's asked to do that. She says the neighborhood isn't great.

And how am I supposed to afford something better? I'm just starting out, for Heaven's sake.

ONE

The next car looked like the first one had, the original car that had started all this. Modern. Glass and aluminum. Graffiti and ads. A car that belonged not to nightmare but to reality – if reality had any meaning left to them.

To Jim was almost depressing in a way, as though the train was telling them that no matter how far along they got, they would always end up back where they started.

Adolfa looked around the car as though afraid it might disappear from around them. She muttered something under her breath.

"What was that?" Jim asked. He didn't really care what it was. He said it for something to say, for a way to blank out the terrible sound of Olik's screams, and the worse sound of his daughters' shrieking.

"Spanish," said Adolfa. "Something that means, 'Last to first, first to last.'"

"Sounds like something out of the Bible."

"It is."

She crossed herself and stepped forward, pulling Jim along with her. But only a step or two. Then she started to cough. The cough doubled her over, a chopping, grating hack that sounded wet and slimy, the cough of someone well into serious illness.

Jim put out a steadying hand. "You okay?"

Adolfa nodded, but didn't stop coughing. She kept hacking, and though Jim couldn't see her face, the sliver of her profile that he *could* see turned deep red.

Finally the coughs seemed to dissipate. Adolfa gripped his arm as though the attack had stolen her strength, as though she might keel over. Then she pushed herself fully upright. She was panting.

"You sure you're all right?"

She nodded, gulped, nodded again. "Maybe I will sit down for a moment," she said.

Jim led her to one of the plastic seats that jutted like shiny tumors out of the walls of the subway car.

"At least the lights are on again," he said.

Adolfa nodded and smiled. But the smile crumpled in on itself as another coughing fit seized her halfway to the seat. This one was worse than the first.

After all that had gone before, Jim half expected her head to explode, or some alien parasite to crawl out of her eyes. But she just coughed. It was mundane, almost banal considering all that they had been through.

Just a cough.

And this is how the world ends, he thought insanely. Not with a bang, but with a cough.

Jim looked out the windows. The subway seemed to be traveling faster than ever, the lights rocketing by at eye-scorching speeds, so fast that they were streaks in the otherwise pure darkness of the tunnel. He wondered what he might see if the train were to slow down enough to allow them a view of their surroundings.

He wondered if he *wanted* to see.

For a moment a part of his mind knew. A part of him understood what was happening. And it screamed deep within him, in a hidden part that kept his darkest moments, his blackest memories. The place that remembered the things that frightened him most, that had made him who he was and had motivated him to seek out people like Carolyn and Maddie, good people who would keep him safe from the evils that seemed to rear themselves at every turn in a wicked world.

Then the knowledge was gone. Gone like the lights that streaked past, dazzling and blinding but too fast to track, too quick to comprehend.

"You all right, *mi hijo*?"

Jim blinked. He was staring at the darkness beyond the window glass. How long had he been lost in thought, in almost-comprehension? He didn't know. He looked at Adolfa. She was still red, still panting, so it couldn't have been too long.

He forced a smile. "Isn't that my line?" He sat next to her and put an arm around her shoulder. "Are *you* okay?"

Adolfa tried to smile. No cough this time but the smile still died before it was properly born. She shrugged. "Not sure I'll ever be okay again." Her body shivered, a shudder so severe it was nearly a convulsion. "What happened to Olik...."

Jim nodded. He squeezed Adolfa's shoulder. "I know."

"Will that happen to us?"

"I don't know." How could he know? How could any of them know what was going to happen next, if none of them knew what was going on around them?

Sorta like life.

Jim frowned. He didn't like that train of thought. Life was a good thing. It *meant* something. There was more to it than just pain and fear. So he wasn't going to fall into a pit of cynicism and permanent angst just because of what was happening right now.

What about because of what happened before? *What happened to* her? *To* all of them?

No. No. NO!

"Jim? Jim?!"

Again he blinked. Again he didn't know how long his mind had been away. Lost in thought and in a burgeoning madness that crept ever closer, ever closer. The subway seemed to be dragging him to it. Last Stop: *Insanity.*

"We have to get off this thing," he said.

"I'd love that," said Adolfa. "Any ideas?"

He looked around. The car presented nothing new. Seats. Poles. Ads.

A map.

He got up. He went to it.

Like the map that they had seen in the earlier car, this one bore only the barest resemblance to a typical New York subway route map. The colors, the symbols – even the lettering itself – were all wrong.

But there was one thing he understood. A black "X" that all the routes now seemed to run to. And above it:

"**LAST STOP.**" His thought of a moment ago seemed suddenly prescient.

Last Stop: Insanity.

He shivered, then forced his mind away from that idea. There had to be an answer here.

Below the words "**LAST STOP**" there were other letters in languages he didn't understand. But though he didn't understand them, he got a definite chill looking at them. A sense of finality.

No, not just finality. Oblivion. Like the stop meant not merely an end to the train's forward motion, but to *everything.* As though eternity itself would end in the moment the subway car pulled into that station.

And next to the "X," next to the "**LAST STOP**" marker... a dot.

It was moving.

"Is that us?" said Adolfa. She had gotten up and now stood beside him. And Jim could tell from the breathy quality of her voice that she, too, felt his fear, felt the terror that he felt. The sense that whatever happened when the train reached its final destination would make everything that had happened before seem like a pleasant daydream in comparison.

The dot phased into a position a tiny bit closer to the **LAST STOP**.

"Is that us?" repeated the old woman.

"Yes," said Jim. "I think it is."

TWO

Adolfa let a small scream escape, then began running frantically around the subway car. She pushed on the windows, pulled at the door at the front of the car. None of it opened. None of it offered a way out.

Jim didn't move. He just watched the dot, the dot that was them, moving ever closer to the point that represented... what?

Again he knew. For a moment, an instant, he *knew*. Then the moment was past and again his mind was in darkness.

I'm coming Carolyn. I'm coming Maddie. I promise.

He hoped it wasn't a lie.

Adolfa coughed again. This time the coughing became a damp retching. She bent over and clutched at her stomach, and when she stood twin streams of blood ran from her nostrils.

Jim went to her. "Hey, you're bleeding." He pulled a handkerchief from his pocket. He dabbed at the blood but it wouldn't stop. "Sit down." He guided the old lady to a seat.

"Damn," she whispered. Her voice bubbled around the blood, making her sound like she was drowning.

She looked at Jim, and he recoiled. "What?" she said.

He shook his head. He didn't know how to answer her. Where only a moment before she had seemed like a healthy older woman, suddenly her flesh was sagging, changing. The skin of her face seemed like it was no longer attached to her skull, drooping strangely and giving her the appearance of someone who had suffered a severe stroke.

"What?" Adolfa said again. "What ish it?" Her voice was slurring, and at the end of the question she unleashed another flurry of coughs.

Tic... tictictic... tic....

Jim looked down automatically, his eyes tracking the sound of something plinking against the metal floor of the subway car. He didn't see what had made the sound for a moment, his eyes tracking wildly left and right and up and down without spotting anything. Then he saw them: splashes of red with white centers.

Blood. Blood and... *teeth.*

He looked back at Adolfa. Her face was still sagging, the skin loosening ever further. And now her baglike chin was covered in blood, both from her still-sluicing nostrils and from the blood drooling thinly from her mouth. From the holes where many of her teeth had been.

As Jim watched, Adolfa reached with shaking fingers into her mouth and plucked out a molar. Jim knew – he *knew*, dammit – that Adolfa had been possessed of a wide, pleasant, white smile. But the tooth that she pulled out was yellow and rotted. It was the tooth of someone who had been drinking cola for years and hadn't ever bothered with brushing her teeth in the interim.

A fresh gout of blood spurted over Adolfa's lips when she pulled the rotten tooth out of her jaw. She didn't seem to notice. She laughed. The laugh was bereft of humor, the laugh that takes over when horror has reached such an extreme that the only choices are to laugh or to allow oblivion to claim you.

"What'sh going on?" she said. The words still bubbled, and another tooth pushed its way out of her mouth with the sound. Her skin had sagged so far that her eyes were almost invisible, displaced by the strange change in her facial layout. Her nasal bones poked through skin that Jim was fairly sure had once covered Adolfa's forehead. The effect was less gory than much of what he had seen on the subway, but more sickening in a strange way. As though seeing a human pulled apart bit by bit was less offensive to nature than merely watching it adjusted by a few inches.

Adolfa patted herself. Her dress, which before had fit her well, now hung loosely. Her breasts had become dangling sacks of flesh, low and sickly. Her thighs had become visibly thinner, and yet what flesh remained of them was all fatty tissue. She had no muscle tone left, like a calf that had been raised in a too-small cage for the sole purpose of being slaughtered for veal.

Adolfa started to cry. "Thish can't be happening to me," she said. "Not to me. Not to *me*."

She sagged. Jim caught her. His flesh crawled. He liked Adolfa. But in that moment he wished that someone – anyone – else could have been there to catch her. What had happened to her was too unsettling, too grotesque.

"Adolfa?" he said after a moment.

There was no answer.

And Jim wondered if he was the only one left in the subway.

THREE

A moment later Adolfa sat up again. Not dead after all. Jim was relieved. He hadn't been able to get up the courage to check for a pulse, or even to listen closely for breath. He hadn't wanted to get that close to her. To whatever she had become.

"You're awake."

Adolfa snuffled. He thought she might start crying again, but she held it together. Her face had stopped sliding off her bones, but now strange sores had appeared on it. They were crusty and painful-looking, scabrous tissue that oozed pus and blood. They clustered around the old woman's mouth especially, and the first time she tried to talk a number of them cracked open and seeped into her mouth.

"What I deserve," she whispered.

"What?" said Jim.

"What we all deserve."

Jim shook his head. "I don't understand." He thought Adolfa must be delirious. Whatever sickness she had contracted must be giving her a fever. Maybe she was hallucinating.

"This place," she said. "It's taking us to what we deserve."

"I don't think so," Jim said.

Adolfa clutched at him with fingers that suddenly seemed to have the power of a dozen strong men. "It's true," she whispered. Blood sprayed out of her mouth. Jim felt it speckle his face, and gorge rose up in his throat. "Each car is for one of us. To punish one of us. Freddy. Xavier. Karen. Olik. The doors didn't open in each car until one person had died." She swallowed, grimacing in pain. "This car must be mine."

She started coughing again. More blood poured from her mouth. Her body slumped, as though all the strength had gone from her.

Jim caught her. "Adolfa, don't be silly. You're an *abuelita*, a shop keeper. Why would anyone want to punish you?"

Adolfa pushed herself up a bit. Her drooping eyes focused on his. She laughed. Then the laugh turned into a cackle. "A shop keeper?" The cackle increased in volume, growing hysterical. "A *shop keeper*?" She coughed. Blood. She inhaled, coughed more. Then seemed to stop the hacking coughs by force of will. She smiled, the grin a horrific sight in the sagging mask of her face. "I took over the family business when my husband died," she said. "Selling drugs. The largest cartel of cocaine, heroine, and meth in seven countries." Another cough. Another gout. "I was in New York to negotiate a new market, a business agreement with a rival family."

Jim shook his head. He didn't believe that. "No," he said. "Adolfa, this is insane."

Her face was drooping more now. Her eyes were lost, gone from the folds of skin that bore no relation to the place they should have been. "Insane?" She laughed. "A pedophile, a skin-merchant, a rapist, a killer, a drug dealer." She grew suddenly serious. "No, we all deserve this, *mi hijo*." She started to sag again. "This is my car. This is my place to go." Jim caught her. She looked at him. "It is only you I do not understand, *mi hijo*. The only good man in a den of thieves and killers." She touched his cheek. The beds of her nails were ruptured, star hemorrhages that oozed bloody trails across his skin. "Perhaps you were here to bear witness. To give final rites and comfort to the damned."

Adolfa's fingers fell away from his cheeks. She slumped forward and Jim lowered her to the gently rocking floor of the still-rocketing subway train.

Click-clack click-clack click-clack.

Adolfa's face was an amorphous mass, gone, lost in folds of featureless flesh. Her bony body started to twitch.

"Adolfa?"

She began to convulse. Somewhere from within the folds of what had once been her face, a muffled scream sounded. Her body flopped like a fish.

The door at the front of the car slid open.

Jim looked down at Adolfa. Looked at her like he had looked at someone long before.

(*so much blood. so much blood.*)

Then he stood. Walked toward the open door.

Adolfa was lost.

He had to get off this train. Had to get home, had to get to his girls.

FOUR

The open door beckoned at the front of the subway car. Jim could only hope that what Adolfa had said was true – that he was here to bear some sort of horrific witness, a dark apostle to an evil gospel, and that now the others were gone he would be free to go.

He cast a last backward look at Adolfa. She was still seizing, her frail body thrashing against the floor, her feet tapping and rapping and her shoulders thumping as she twitched her way back and forth across the center aisle. How long would it take her to die? Jim didn't know.

He turned back to the door.

And there were two people standing there. A man and a woman. They were tall. Good-looking. They were in their mid-thirties, both blondes with blue eyes that looked at him for only the barest instant before they stepped into the car.

The door shut behind them.

Jim's heart lurched. This wasn't right. This wasn't the way it was supposed to go, the way it *had* gone. He was supposed to get *out* of here. What was happening now? What new awfulness was about to descend on him?

The man and woman stepped toward him. Jim fell back a step, sure that they would attack him, certain that they were the next wave of terror sent to torment him.

But they took no notice of him. They stepped past him. Went to the still-stuttering form of Adolfa. They knelt beside her. The blonde woman cradled Adolfa's head – what was left of her head, the deformed mass of skin and bone that her head had become – in her lap. The young man passed his hands over her spasming body.

Jim watched, transfixed, as Adolfa's body stopped convulsing. It relaxed so fully and completely he thought at first she must be dead. Then he realized that her dress was rising and falling, rhythmically and regularly. She was breathing.

And looking at her breathing, Jim saw with amazement that her body had filled out again. It was returning to its previous health.

"Who are you?" he said.

Neither the man nor the woman paid any attention to him. He wondered if they were angels. But they couldn't be, could they? Not if they were come to save an admitted drug dealer, especially if they were doing so in lieu of saving someone whose girls were waiting for him, depending on him.

"What's going on?" he said a moment later. Still no answer.

Adolfa's face shifted. It pulled back to its moorings on the bone below. It began to resemble itself again. The blood seemed to seep into the skin and disappear. The rotten teeth that remained in her mouth grew bright and white once more, and the gaps where no teeth were suddenly held molars and incisors and bicuspids again.

The old woman opened her eyes.

"Adolfa!" Jim said.

Adolfa didn't seem to notice him. She looked up at the man and woman who knelt beside her, who held her in their arms and who had brought her back from doom's door. Her eyes moved from the man to the woman, and back again. "Scott," she said. "Kim."

"Hello, *Mamá*," said Kim, and Jim remembered Adolfa telling him, several cars and forever ago, about her son marrying a girl and bringing her into the family business.

"You came for me," said Adolfa, and pulled Kim down into a hug. Kim didn't return the hug, only seeming to endure it. After a moment, Adolfa let go. "What?" she said. "What is it?"

Kim and Scott exchanged a look that spoke of untold secrets. Finally Scott, in a curiously emotionless voice, said, "You were supposed to die."

"What?" said Adolfa.

"You kept living," said Kim. "Kept living and living, just getting older and older and never dying. Never dying."

"So we had to hire someone," said Scott.

"To help you along," said Kim. Both of them spoke strangely, almost like they were being *made* to speak, as if the words were coming forth against their will.

"What do you mean?" said Adolfa.

"You know what we mean," said Kim.

243

"It's why Karen was here," said Scott.

Jim started. But he remembered. Remembered Karen grabbing Adolfa and saying she was here for the old lady; something about her "commission." He gaped. Had Adolfa's family *hired* her?

Adolfa must have been thinking the same thing, because her face registered shock. Then disappointment.

Then rage.

"You *hijos de* –" she began. But never finished.

Kim waved, and the aluminum poles nearest Adolfa detached from the ceiling. They writhed like snakes, suddenly flexible, then as Jim watched they seemed to shift in appearance. No longer aluminum poles, now they resembled tubing. The bottoms were still anchored in the floor, but the tops glinted. Like something sharp.

Needles.

The pole/tubes shot out, and wrapped themselves around Adolfa's arms and legs. Another one trussed around her neck. The needles at the ends of the tubes buried themselves in her wrists and thighs and chin. Then the tubes darkened as something flowed through them... and into Adolfa.

Her body convulsed again. The skin pulled from its bones. The sores reappeared, and blood poured from every orifice on her body. She screamed.

Jim edged away from the scene. His only hope was to get away before the homicidal relatives of the old drug dealer noticed he was there.

He glanced at the front door.

It was still closed.

Adolfa shrieked again. Her scream bubbled around skin that had the consistency of loose putty. Jim looked back at her.

And saw that Kim and Scott were staring right at him.

FIVE

Jim held up his hands. "Please," he said. Hot tears burned behind his eyes. "I don't know what's going on, but I don't belong here." He glanced over his shoulder. The door was still closed.

He looked back. Scott and Kim were still kneeling beside Adolfa. Still staring at him. Adolfa was screaming, and the scream burrowed like a tick into the deepest parts of his mind, shaking loose everything that he had ever suffered or hoped to bury there.

Kim and Scott looked at each other. Then back at Jim.

"I have a family waiting for me. I don't belong here." Jim pointed at Adolfa as she flailed on the floor. "She said it herself."

Kim looked at Scott. "Should we kill him?" she said. Her voice still sounded queer.

Scott nodded. "I think so."

They looked at Jim. He flicked one more glance over his shoulder. The door was still shut. And he knew that it was because this car hadn't claimed its victim yet. Hadn't claimed its due.

He ran. Not toward the door – that would have been useless – but toward Scott. Toward Kim.

Toward Adolfa.

As he ran, he reached toward his pocket. Not for his journal, though. His hand veered aside at the last second. He pulled something from his waistband.

Xavier's knife.

Kim and Scott reached for Jim.

He dodged their hands.

He dropped down. Looked at Adolfa's spasming body. "You were right about me," he whispered. "I really am a good person. And I don't belong here."

And then he drew the knife across the old woman's throat. It was a perfect, practiced cut. Carotids and jugular were severed in an instant.

Jim felt the fingers of Kim and Scott on his arms and shoulders. And felt them changing. Claws emerging, flesh growing scaly and hard.

But at the same time, the blood from Adolfa's body spattered against the floor of the subway car. At the same time, the lifeblood splashed from her in a gout.

At the same time, the door at the front of the car opened.

At the same time, Jim ran.

Fingers grabbed for him, tearing his shirt from his back. They raked bloody furrows in his flesh. But then the things that Kim and Scott had become turned to lap up the blood that still spilled on the metal floor.

Adolfa screamed, sputtered, gurgled. An impossible sound through her cut throat, but still she made it. Her skin fell from her bones, her body emptied of blood. But still she screamed. As Freddy had screamed, as Xavier and Karen and Olik had screamed. She screamed though dead, a wail of never-ending pain and betrayal and agony.

Jim threw himself through the door. Nothing followed him. Nothing but the scream.

And the subway continued on.

1 FARE

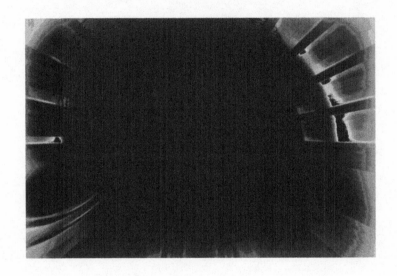

Got in a fight with Carolyn today. Stupid fight about nothing. Maddie heard it. She cried.

I'll make it up to her. To both of them. After work today. We'll go on a picnic.

ONE

Jim pushed through the doors to the next car. The scream, Adolfa's scream, followed him. Followed him like a bloodhound that has caught the scent of a lifetime. Like a stink that would not be shaken loose.

Like past sins.

He ran into the next car. And blinked with surprise as silence fell with the power and finality of a hammer blow.

All was quiet.

All was dark.

He couldn't see anything, couldn't hear anything, couldn't feel anything.

Then a single light shone. A moonbeam, a pure white shaft of light that fell on the face of an angel.

His mother.

Jim looked down at himself. His hands were his hands. His hands and yet *not* his hands. His body, yet *not* his body. It was all different, yet all the same.

He held a knife. But not Xavier's knife –

(*who's Xavier? where did that thought come from?*)

– no, this was just an ordinary kitchen knife, taken from the block on the counter next to the white stove that Mother always kept spotless.

He crept to her. He walked on feet that were bare, silent on a floor that had somehow become wood –

(*wasn't it metal just a moment ago?*)

– laminate, a light color by day but dark and pooled in shadow now, in the deepest part of the night.

Jim was quiet. Quiet as a mouse, quiet as any animal in any of the bedtime stories that Mother had ever read to him. But still she opened her eyes when he stood by her. Maybe that was part of being a mother. Maybe there was some extra sense given to parents that allowed them to know when their children were near, even in their sleep.

Jim didn't understand it, but he accepted it. It didn't matter.

Mother smiled off the cobwebs of sleep. She reached for him. "Jimmy, you okay?" she said. "Did you have a bad dream?"

Jim shook his head. "No."

"Then what is it?" Concern on her face. Her beautiful face.

Jim leaned in. "You know how I took extra lemon drops without asking?"

She smiled. "Sorry I got mad."

"I'm sorry, too," he said.

"It's okay." She started to pull him in for a hug.

He resisted. "No. I'm not sorry for taking the candy. Just that you reacted so badly."

The first cut surprised her. She didn't scream, just sort of inhaled, a "hah?" sound that excited his eleven-year-old brain on a level he hadn't been aware of previously.

The second cut went into her throat. Not fatal, not right away. But it tired her quickly. Her blood pumped out, soaked the sheets and the mattress.

After that she got weaker and weaker. Jim was able to grab the knife with both hands and plunge it into her repeatedly. Chest. Legs. Arms. She didn't scream. Just made a strange noise, a surprised, pained groan.

"Ung-ung-ung," she said. Jim listened to the sound. He smiled. It was the sound of an early inheritance. Of no one telling him to go to bed early, to eat his greens. It was the sound of what he wanted, when he wanted.

He decided then that that would be his job, his vocation, his profession: to have what he wanted, to take what he needed. An no one would tell him otherwise, no one would tell him no. He would have what he wanted. He deserved it. He was special.

Hadn't Mother always told him so?

She was staring at him. Looking at him with eyes that looked so betrayed, so hurt. Which he didn't understand, because he was doing the responsible thing, the *only* thing.

He used the knife again. Blood pooled in her eyesockets when he was done. She thrashed a bit, but not much. And she wasn't looking at him like that anymore.

Jim ran away while she was still bleeding, still thrashing. He wiped off the knife first, leaving it beside her. Tears were in his eyes, he was crying hysterically. He would be found in the woods near the house in a few hours. The poor, traumatized boy who found his mother's body after she was savagely murdered by a robber. He had already stolen and hidden several of her jewels, and he broke some panes of glass on the way out of the house.

It was perfect.

No one would ever know.

It was what he had to do. What he needed.

He ran through the door. Ran into the woods. Into the strobing lights of fireflies and winking stars.

The night swallowed him.

TWO

Jim blinked. The woods were gone. The trees and the house of his childhood had melted back into the mists of happily hidden memory. He looked at his hands, half-expecting to see them the smooth, white hands of a sixth-grader again. Half-expecting to see them blanketed in his mother's blood.

They were his own hands. The hands of a middle-aged man. And the blood on them was not his mother's. It was Adolfa's.

A clapping sound jogged his attention back to the present. To wherever or whenever or whatever place he had found himself trapped in.

It was the man. The driver. The too-thin person in the New York transit outfit who had started all this, who had been the harbinger of this nightmare. He was standing in the middle of the subway car – what must be the *first* subway car, the *final* subway car – and clapping derisively.

"Very nicely done, Jim," said the man. He had a New York accent, a hint of the Bronx that went perfectly with his outfit. "You made it here, you made it the farthest. Kudos, cheers, and huzzah to you, my friend." He blew a raspberry in the air, a silly noise that somehow sounded obscene in this place.

The clapping suddenly felt like daggers against Jim's ears. He needed it to stop. Rage rose up, red and dangerous, in his mind.

"You did this to me," he said.

"Not at all," said the gaunt man. He kept clapping. Louder now, the clapping sounded like thunder.

"You *did this to me!*" Jim shrieked, and rushed at the driver. He held Xavier's knife in front of him, like a divining rod that hungered for blood, that could only be quenched by the sanguine taste of life pumping along its length.

The driver watched him come. He kept clapping. Kept clapping. Kept clapping.

Jim screamed, a wordless scream of mad frustration. This wasn't fair! He had tried so hard, so many years of doing what he had to to get ahead, so many years of work and effort to get to where he had a family, a life. His girls.

And now this man, this bastard was going to get in his way.

The knife reached for the driver. Questing for his blood.

The driver reached out, his hands pushing forward as though he hungered to be pricked by the blade. As he did so, his face changed. The skin puckered and then fell away in a bloody sheet. Only bone was left behind: the skull that Jim had seen at the front of the subway train before he stepped on the last car.

The driver's hand, also bereft of flesh, continued reaching for the knife. Finger bones clicked around the blade. Jim's hand stopped moving, its forward motion arrested as perfectly and completely as if he had run into a brick wall. *He* couldn't stop, though. Not completely. He kept running forward, momentum driving him onward and folding his body around the knife and the hand that held it, his breath forced out of him with an explosive puff.

Then he rebounded, his feet slipping on the metal floor of the car. He fell. And realized that there was warmth seeping across his pants.

He looked up.

The skeleton in the transit outfit was still holding the knife. It was smiling. "Fair's fair, Jim," it said.

Jim looked down. There was a long gash along his forearm, a vertical slit that was pumping blood at an alarming rate.

"What...?" he began. "What did you do?"

The skull clicked its teeth together. "You've been a smart one, haven't you?"

Jim looked up at the thing, at the beast that had come for him. "I don't know what you mean," he said defiantly, even as a terrifying coldness seeped into his arms and legs.

The skull leaned in close. "Oh, don't you?" it said. And in the dark holes of its eyes Jim thought he saw something writhing, like a nest of snakes being born and being eaten in a never-ending cycle of blood and death.

The demon driver touched a single fleshless finger to Jim's chest. He felt it like an icepick, burrowing into his heart. He screamed and felt...

Memory.

Looking at Karen, worrying she might go insane. That she might lose it. "Okay," he said, "how about I care because if you go nuts that's one more thing I have to worry about in here?" And she thought he was kidding. That he was really worried about her as a person. But he wasn't kidding. He wanted – needed – her to live. Needed them all to live. Because the more people who survived, the more bodies there were to provide him with cover.

Olik wasn't the only one who knew how to sleep when wolves were around....

And then he was in a different place. Grinding the gun into Karen's head, telling himself he couldn't let her get away from the door because there wasn't time. But there was time. There was always time. He just didn't want to be the one to put his hands out the door, didn't want to be the one to be in harm's way if there was someone else to do that work....

Another place. Pulling Adolfa away from gunfire as Karen pulled the trigger on the micro-Uzi. Only now there was no disguising what he was doing. There was no charity there, no philanthropy. He just pulled her in front of him. He wasn't pulling her to safety, he was using her as a shield....

Then back in the dark subway, the skull staring at him with those terrible dark eyes.

"Everything you did was for you," said the skull. "You understood the evil around you not because you were a psychiatrist –"

"I never said I *was*," said Jim. He was almost gasping. Desperation coloring his voice.

"No, you carefully avoided that." The skull grinned horribly. "As though not lying at this point might help you." The Bronx voice laughed. It touched Jim in the chest again, and again the pain was bright and terrible. "But you didn't need to be a shrink, pal, didja? Because you already knew about the kinds of people you were dealing with. You had *been* all of those people, hadn't you?" The pain in Jim's chest was almost too much to bear, but somehow grew worse.

"Why me?" he asked. His voice was almost a whimper, a weak version of the strength it had once been.

The driver seemed to find that oh-so-amusing. "My kingdom for a hypocrite," it said with a chuckle. "Why you?" It touched Jim's head. Again came the pain like someone had taken a blowtorch to his exposed nerve endings.

"Freddy was a pedophile," whispered the skull. "So he went first. Because you can't let things like that stay around."

And now Jim saw. Saw what Freddy had seen: the children that came to him in the first car, that crowded around him and surrounded him. "Make them stop touching me," said Freddy the Perv. "They're touching me, make them stop," he said in much the same way that those children had said when he touched them, when he molested them and destroyed their innocence. And no one saw them, no one saw their pain. Just as no one saw them now, when they came to exact their revenge. No one had seen or believed the children he had savaged in life, so it was only just that no one see them come for their vengeance. No one saw them as they pulled apart the fingers that had touched

259

them, as they tore away the lips that had kissed them, as they destroyed him one cell at a time... knowing that he would find himself back in the car soon, ready for them to minister to him once again.

Jim gasped. Back in the subway car but for a moment before the skull, the driver who commanded this strange world, said, "But what's worse, I wonder: a pedophile or a serial rapist?"

Xavier. The things invading him. Like phalluses forcing into his secret places. "Get it outta me! Get it outta me!" And then a creature, born of sin and shame and rape most foul, a creature that he would bear and that would destroy him in its birthing. And that in turn would become him and his legacy, a microcosm of a tragedy played out so many times in so many places all over the world. A tragedy still being played out, just as Xavier was still being born and pulled apart by his seed, and born and dying and born and dying into infinity.

"For that was his punishment," whispered the skull. Its finger twisted against Jim's skin, bringing fresh agony.

Karen. A woman whose only life was death. A name in an anonymous inbox, a sum in a Cayman Islands account, and she would end a life. There was no emotion in her, no life in her own heart. She had killed many – had come to kill Adolfa, on the last day of her own life. Hired by Scott and Kim, who had grown tired of waiting for the old bitch to die so they could take over the "family business." The hit had gone wrong, she had taken three bullets from Adolfa's bodyguard – or thought she had, before finding herself somehow aboard the subway platform. But she took it as a sign. And another sign when Adolfa was there, too. She could complete the job. Could earn her commission.

But every person she had ever slain had appeared on her tablet. Had named her for what she was. A murderer. Her hands had run red with their blood, blood that would never come clean, would never be anything but bright against her skin.

Then they had come for her – even the little girl she'd killed for a jealous mistress – and dragged her off the subway. And now she was one with them, experiencing the pain of their lives, cut short for eternity.

"Stop," whispered Jim.

"No," said the driver. "This doesn't stop. That's the point."

Another twist. Another pain.

Olik. A man who went from pornography in his own country to a thriving international internet pornography business to a lively trade in the sex slave industry. So many families broken as he took their daughters, and sometimes sons, to quench the appetites of others. It was only appropriate that he should see his own daughters fall to the same urges. That he should have his head hung on a pole to watch their defilement forever.

Jim was crying. Screaming as more pain came.

Adolfa. A sweet old lady who runs the family business. Overseeing accounting. New "product." And running the competition out of business — and into the ground. So her punishment is to spend forever in the pain she inflicted on countless addicts. Watched over by her own "loving family," who will wait forever for her to die, not out of love, but out of greed. Selling her to buy the drugs she has built, just as so many others sold their sons, their daughters, their own flesh for the wares she offered.

She has no hope of respite. For she has reduced human suffering to a question of how much money can be gleaned before dissolution.

And in the subway, dissolution never comes.

Jim shook his head. "No," he said. "This isn't fair. It isn't fair." He looked up at the skull. "What about my girls?"

The skull's grin widened. "What *about* your girls?" And it touched him one more time.

THREE

The argument. Such a silly thing.

He couldn't understand how it had gotten to this point.

But here it was. Here *they* were.

Carolyn was staring at him, holding Maddie tightly to her, as though she were afraid he was going to *hurt* her, for God's sake.

"Come on, Carolyn," Jim said. He took a step toward her.

"Don't you come any closer," she shouted. Her voice was terrified, which made him feel just awful. Couldn't she see how much she and Maddie *meant* to him?

He stopped moving. He didn't need to run after them, anyway. They were in their bathroom, huddled in the tub. Nowhere for them to go, really. "Carolyn, please. Let's just talk this out."

"I don't even *know who you are.*"

That stung. "How can you not know me?" he said, dumbfounded. "I've known you two for months. Forever, it feels like." He hazarded another small step forward. "I love you. You're my girls."

"*What?*"

"I know everything about you. I know that you love banana bread but hate bananas, Carolyn. I know that your favorite place in the world is Disneyland, Maddie. That you both want to live in a treehouse like the Swiss Family Robinson someday. So how can you say you don't know me?"

Carolyn's face changed. His heart leapt, sure at first that she was coming around, that she was remembering – was *realizing* who he was and that they were his girls. But then he saw confusion in her eyes. "How do you know those things?" she said. "Where did you...?" Then the confusion disappeared. "Oh my God. Tom's journal."

Jim shook his head. The conversation wasn't going how he had planned. "Carolyn, let's not –"

"We thought he lost it at the park, but you *stole it*. You stole it and, what? You fixated on us? On me and Maddie?"

The little girl whimpered in her mother's arms. Jim's heart fell. He didn't want her to feel bad. That would just kill him.

"No, Carolyn, I just... I knew you were...." The words weren't coming. "You're my girls," he finally said.

"And for that *you killed my husband?*" screamed Carolyn.

Jim didn't look behind him. Didn't look at the body on the bed. He knew from past experience that that wouldn't help anything. The key was to move forward. To get past what was past and focus on the future that could be, the future he *deserved*.

He stepped toward them. One more step and he could grab her. Could grab Carolyn, could grab Maddie. He'd been wanting to hold them since he saw them in the park almost a year ago. If he could just hold them, he could make them understand. He knew he could.

If he could just hold them.

One more step.

He reached out.

"You sonofabitch," said Carolyn.

That stopped him up short. "Honey, let's watch our language in front of Maddie."

Her mouth curled. Jim took another step.

Carolyn pulled something out from behind Maddie. "Sonofabitch," she said again. There was a loud sound, three claps of thunder. Maddie screamed. Something punched Jim against the back wall of the bathroom. He slid to the floor.

Carolyn stood. Holding Maddie in one hand. A dark weapon in her other one. Jim couldn't make out what it was: everything was getting dark.

"Why'd you do that?" he said. "I can't feel my legs." He giggled.

"Go to hell," said Carolyn. She aimed the weapon at his face.

Thunder rolled once more.

FOUR

Jim felt the pain of the bony fingers on his skin, and now he recognized them as what they were: the pain of bullets raining down on him.

The skull grinned at him. "I saved you for the end because you were the worst," it said. "Pedophiles, drug dealers, skin traders, rapists, killers. They steal your life, your body. But sociopaths, people like you... they hide beside you, they pretend to be your friends. Then they steal your soul."

The side doors of the subway train opened.

"You pride yourself on being a good man," said the skull. The driver. "You even believe it. But being a good man is easy if your test for goodness is doing whatever you want, *taking* what you want. Regardless of who else it hurts."

Through the doors on one side, a woman entered. Tall, beautiful. Kind. She was dressed in a nightgown. She had no eyes.

"Mother?" said Jim.

Through the other doors, a girl and her daughter. One dark, one light. Jim felt a thrill of hope as they came into the car.

They're here to save me, he thought.

But as they stepped forward, they seemed to shift for a moment. For an instant they weren't his girls. No, they were two creatures whose humanity had long since disappeared, if ever it had existed in the first place. Their faces were scaly and cold, the expressionless visages of snakes., They each had three mouths, and those mouths were lined with sawlike teeth that gnashed together in eternal hunger.

Their legs were short, and ended in hooves.

Then the moment ended, and Jim saw his girls again. But he knew it as a lie. It wasn't Maddie, it wasn't Carolyn. It wasn't his mother coming toward him. Just as it hadn't been Olik's children being savaged in the car, hadn't been the girls and boys whom Olik sold that came to wreak vengeance upon him. It wasn't Adolfa's family in the car with her, waiting forever for her to die; and it wasn't really the children that Freddy had molested who were now cavorting forever on his sentient, pain-ridden remains.

The only things here were beings that had been born here, and would exist forever in a place meant only to bring pain and shame.

As if to give lie to Jim's thoughts, Maddie spoke. "Hello, Daddy," she said. She licked her lips, and her tongue was black and subtly forked.

"Hello, my love," said his mother. She was holding something. It was a knife. A kitchen knife from the block near the stove. The stove she kept so clean, so spotless.

The driver stepped back to give room to the newcomers. They crowded around Jim.

His mother reached out for him with fingers that had grown nails ragged and deadly and sharp. They raked over Jim's face, clawed out his eyes. But he could still see. Could see clearly for the first time.

And what he saw terrified him.

He began to scream.

And screamed still louder as the knife began to dance across his skin, as his blood painted the inside of the subway car.

After a long time the driver moved to the front of the car.

Jim could see it move. Could see the skull-thing. It threw one last smile over its shoulder as little Maddie pulled each of Jim's fingers off with delicate joy.

Jim shrieked.

The door at the front of the car opened.

The driver left.

The door closed.

And Jim knew the subway would continue, as his screams and suffering would continue. As justice would continue.

Forever.

Epilogue:
NEW FARES

ONE...

Kayla tried to calm down. One last look over her shoulder to make sure.

No cops. Looked like she'd gotten away.

She didn't know about Frank or Killian, though. The alarm went off at the bank, the cops showed up and started shooting, things went a bit haywire.

Screw 'em.

A moment later she felt a familiar push-pull as the subway drove into the station. The train creaked forward. Stopped.

She walked to the nearest car, the second from the back. Waited for the doors to open.

They didn't.

Weird.

Kayla looked in the car. She could see people in there. A white-bread looking dude, a gangster with some kill-tats on his face. A huge white guy, a little old *latina* lady, a beautiful woman who looked like she was on her way home from her brokerage job, and some pervy type in a stained brown trench coat.

Kayla waved and motioned that the doors weren't opening. None of the half dozen passengers took notice of her. They didn't seem to be ignoring her, but almost seemed like they weren't even *seeing* her. Like they were existing in some other dimension. It was weird, and it gave her the heebie-jeebies.

Someone bustled past her. It was a squirrely guy with a bad combover. "I think the back door is the only one that works," he said in a voice that matched his body: all high and desperate.

"Thanks," she said.

For a moment she considered skipping this train. If the doors didn't open, what else might not be working? She looked at the people in the car in front of her. Shivered.

Then she remembered the cops. They were still on her. They had to be. She had to get moving. The subway was the best way to get going.

She'd just take it to the next stop.

She got on.

A moment later, the doors closed.

And the subway continued on.

ABOUT THE AUTHOR

Michaelbrent Collings is an award-winning screenwriter and novelist. He has written numerous bestselling horror, thriller, sci-fi, and fantasy novels, including *Apparition, The Haunted, Hooked: A True Faerie Tale,* and the bestselling YA series *The Billy Saga.* Follow him on Facebook or on Twitter @mbcollings.

And if you liked *Darkbound,* please leave a review on your favorite book review site... and tell your friends!

Made in the USA
Coppell, TX
27 June 2020